Surrendering Time Se...

# Engaged

## Surrendering the Future

### Julie Arduini

# Engaged: Surrendering the Future

Julie Arduini

Published by Surrendered Scribe Media, Youngstown, Ohio, 44514
http://juliearduini.com

## The Surrendering Time Series

**Entrusted:** Surrendering the Present is a **FREE eRead** at http://juliearduini.com or purchase on Amazon.

**Entangled:** Surrendering the Past is available for purchase on Amazon.

**Engaged:** Surrendering the Future is what you're reading now!

**Finding Freedom Through Surrender**---A 30 Day Devotional, takes the themes and characters from the series to encourage *your* surrender journey. Available for purchase on Amazon.

**Stay in touch** with me through http://juliearduini.com, **follow me on Amazon and Goodreads to learn about free book opportunities and giveaways!**

## Dedication:

To the women who prayed this series through, including original prayer covering member Jennifer Pasquale. Until we reunite in heaven, Bella, Bella.

# Chapter One

Shirley McIlwain and her huge specs enter the Speculator Falls Department Store right before closing. Nothing like a big pair of bug-eye glasses to magnify my troubles.

She saunters down the main aisle, stopping to pick up the black bear figurines and to sniff a vanilla candle. From there, she walks up the slight slope that leads to the clothing section. Where the register is located. And I'm there pretending to read the weekly paper.

*Please don't come over and ask me why I'm back in Speculator Falls.*

As Shirley crosses the threshold and enters the world of sweatshirts, flannel and every kind of Adirondack logo imaginable, she stops near the gloves and picks up a pair, seeming to inspect them as she holds them up to the light. "Do you think you made a mistake?"

I look around and realize it's just us inside the store. I lean closer. "Excuse me?"

She returns the gloves to the stand. "You know, Trish. A mistake."

I clear my throat and walk toward the woman with jet black hair curled under in a style that has to be older than me. "Is it the gloves? I sell the gloves. I don't make them."

Shirley rolls those big eyes of hers. "No. You, Trish. You couldn't wait to leave Speculator Falls for the big city. When you left, the senior center shut down. Remember? Your ex-boyfriend? Poor councilman Ben was so upset with no staff, and he didn't think as a volunteer it was appropriate for me to manage the center. Then there was the reminder of what you did to him, leaving the way you did. Ben made sure he closed the center for what he hoped would be forever."

A line of perspiration slides down my back.

She's not wrong. But talk to Shirley? No thanks.

"All so you could fulfill that dream of yours. But just like that, you returned."

I clench my hands together to control the sudden shakes.

"And in not much more than a year, city girl Trish Maxwell is back in Speculator Falls without a permanent job, helping her mom at the store."

I try to swallow, but my throat catches as the perspiration continues down my backside.

"So I wonder, was leaving here a mistake?"

My eyes start to roll and my knees give out.

⧗⧗⧗

"Trish? Can you hear me?"

A male voice, almost a whisper, is the first thing I hear before I even open my eyes.

But the person I see, close up, is Shirley hovering over me. Those big pupils can really scare a person.

"What's going on?" I try to sit up, but my head collides with Shirley's. A hand lands on my shoulder and presses me down to the floor.

"Trish, I need you to stay down until I've finished examining you. Shirley? Could you do me a favor and give us a little room?"

Shirley disappears, and kneeling before me is Wayne Peterson, Hamilton County paramedic. I didn't know his eyes were Caribbean blue.

"What happened?" Left on the floor, all I'm able to do is gaze into those ocean blues while he flashes a light between mine.

Wayne clicks off the light. "You fainted."

Shirley pipes up from across the room. "Remember? I was asking if you regret leaving the senior center and Speculator Falls for a job in New York that didn't even last a year. Your eyes got really big and then they rolled. Next thing I know, you're on the floor."

Right. The whole mistake question.

A whiff of breezy aftershave dances around my nostrils.

"Have you been sedentary today, Trish?" Wayne places his hand under my back and gently assists me to a sitting position.

I take a deep breath. "It's October in Speculator Falls. Not exactly turning the customers away here." I wave my hand to gesture but feel a stab across my forehead.

Wayne lays a hand to steady me. "Duly noted. What I mean is, did you move a little fast after a period of non-activity? I think your blood pressure dropped and your body reacted."

Ugh. Why didn't I stay behind the counter and let Shirley shop without help?

"Yeah, that sounds about right."

"I called for help immediately. I even put the 'closed' sign on the door so no one would come in," Shirley said.

That basic First Aid class at the senior center apparently did my former assistant some good. "Thanks. I appreciate it."

Wayne Velcro's the blood pressure cuff around me and pumps. When he finishes, he makes direct eye contact. "Everything looks good, but I want to take you to the primary care center and get you looked over. Although your floor is carpeted, you did fall, and I want to make sure you don't have a concussion." He gently pulls on my hand and helps me stand.

"I'll take her." Shirley waves her hand.

"No." I don't want to lose contact with my rescuer. "I mean, I need your help here. Ben's probably next door closing the store. I'm sure he'd help you close here, too."

Shirley looks to Wayne. "Did you bring the bus?"

He raises an eyebrow. "I'm sorry?"

"Ambulance. Can you take her to the medical center?"

Wayne grins and his five o'clock shadow looks completely adorable.

How have I missed him in this small village?

"Gotcha. Ms. McIlwain, you watch too many cop shows. But, sure. I have the SUV. I'll transport her."

He winks and I sigh.

Shirley's incessant questions before I fainted come to mind. Mistake? Shirley has no idea.

The good news about fainting on the job is I did so near the end of the day. The Speculator Falls Primary Care Center's near vacant when Wayne brings me in. A girl walks out with a pink cast on her arm when the nurse calls my name.

"What brings you here this evening?" The woman looks to Wayne, not me.

"This is Trish, Jay Maxwell's daughter. She at the department store when she passed out. I think it was a blood pressure drop."

She glances over at me. "The one who left the senior center for the city?"

So my reputation precedes me.

"And lost her job and is back." It's always fun to talk in third person.

"Well, Trish, let's see how you're doing. Wayne, you on duty?"

He looks to his watch and rakes his fingers through his messed brown hair. "Just off." He turns to me. "But I can wait and take you home."

I inhale, hoping to catch another whiff of that tantalizing cologne.

"Not like I've got anything else to do." Wayne turns on his heel and heads to the small waiting room.

Wayne must've learned tact from Shirley.

Thirty minutes later, the nurse throws open the curtain partition. "Dr. Augustine wants you to follow these instructions. Everything looks okay, including the x-ray, but he wants to make sure you guard against head injury and see your family doctor as soon as possible. Sign here and you're good to go."

I press on the clipboard as I scribble my name and hand the paperwork back to her.

Wayne stands as soon as he sees me. "All set?"

"Yes, thanks. I appreciate your help."

He doesn't guide me to the car, but he opens the passenger door for me, a gesture I haven't experienced since dating Ben Regan. "You live with your parents, right?"

I close my eyes. It sounds so awful to hear it out loud. "Yes."

"Good. That way you won't be alone in case you have any complications. Not that I think you will." He starts the SUV and puts it in drive.

"How about you, Wayne? You kind of arrived in town when I was away. Do you live alone?" Because I don't see a ring on his finger.

He turns onto Route 8. "Kind of."

I raise my eyebrows. "That's mysterious."

He chuckles, a low tone that's music to hear. "I don't mean to be cryptic. It's not a cut and dried answer. I live alone most of the time. However, I have a son. Sometimes he stays with me."

Although it's dark, I turn to look for a hint of laughter or sarcasm. There's none. "Oh. So, you're divorced?"

Another tenor laugh. "Is your name Shirley? You ask a lot of questions."

"Sorry. I don't have a lot of people to talk to these days." Not that I did when I lived here the first time.

"I hear ya. It can get pretty dull during most of my shifts, too. To answer your question, no. I'm not divorced. To head off the next question, never married."

Interesting.

"It's not glamorous, but I became a dad when I was a teen. And I know Shirley gave you some pressure about your choices. You can only imagine how my hometown felt about mine."

If his birthplace is as small as Speculator Falls, I'm sure the news spread from one end of the village to the other in five minutes.

"You probably know my son. He's with his mom and step-dad a lot. Noah Peterson. Carla Marshall is his mom."

A flash of a young man with Carla and Will Marshall at church comes to mind. Seems like he had trouble not so long ago, but I can't recall more than that. "That's right."

"This your folk's house?" He points to the Maxwell abode, front porch light on just waiting for me to drag my sorry self inside.

He pulls in the driveway and puts the vehicle in park. "Try not to overdo it."

I open the door and hold up the papers. "I promise I'll follow the instructions."

"Okay. Well, it looks like you're going to be fine."

Until I face Shirley or any of the still furious senior citizens again.

"I think so. Have a good night." I climb out and wave.

I take three steps when I hear my name.

"You know, what Shirley said?"

"Yes?"

"I hope you don't think coming back to Speculator Falls is a mistake."

My laugh exposes my breath and nerves against the cold air.

*Chapter Two*

A sharp pain shoots through the back of my head when a hand rests on my shoulder. I turn and discover Mom standing behind the couch.

"Sorry, Trish, did I scare you?"

Dad turns on the lamp next to the sofa, but it feels like a searchlight. "Shirley called us and told us about your fall. Are you okay, Sweetheart?"

Mom reaches for the afghan I'm wrapped under and pulls on it. "You shouldn't sleep after a head injury, should you?" Her blonde waves bob as she tugs on the blanket.

I rub my eyes as I sit up. "I'm fine. Slight headache is all. Shouldn't you two be the ones sleeping?"

Dad sits next to me. "I wish. Late night. Those lawyer events in Albany seem to last forever. I almost booked a room but I'm glad we didn't. Are you sure you're okay?"

After a few arm, leg and head stretches I nod. "I'm embarrassed more than anything." If the fainting wasn't enough, Wayne Peterson's question about my motives in Speculator Falls was.

Mom places her arm on my forehead. "You don't feel feverish. Shirley assured us Wayne Peterson took good care of you at the primary care center."

"He did a great job. Wayne thinks my blood pressure dropped when I got up too quick. Like I said, embarrassment is the worst of it."

Mom apparently thinks all is well because she leaves the living room and heads to the kitchen. She keeps chatting as she opens the fridge. "Wayne seems nice. I hear he moved here to be closer to his son. Noah."

My parents appear more in the loop than I am.

"That's what he said."

She returns with a cup that looks like it has milk in it and hands it to me. "Sara was at the department store awhile back and was telling me about him. I guess he confessed to Sara that he had been holding onto hope Carla and he could reignite what they had in high school, but Will Marshall won her over. Wayne took it well, Sara said. Even went to Will and Carla's wedding. In return, Carla supported Noah wanting to take on his dad's last name."

Dad reaches for the remote and clicks on the television. "I respect a man who takes responsibility. He seems determined to do the right thing."

Wayne's words to me roll around my mind.

"Speaking of right thing, do you think my life is a mistake?"

Dad pushes the remote, and the television turns dark. TV is dad's way to relax. If it's off, something serious is going on. "Trish, what are you talking about?"

I sigh. "I don't know if Shirley told you, but she was kind of badgering me about my choices. You know, since I came back from New York City, I definitely get the feeling the seniors hate me for leaving and having the center close for a bit. I was so bent on leaving this place and becoming something in a big city. I never thought about the destruction I'd leave behind just taking a job and moving. I hurt a lot of people. She asked if I thought I made a mistake doing all I did. After all, it's not like my move lasted."

Mom sits across from us in her favorite recliner. "Honey. Seniors are set in their ways. They resist change. My guess is they admire you for trying something they wouldn't feel comfortable doing themselves. Besides, it all worked out. Sara made sure the center reopened, they got Jenna as a director, and honestly, the center is thriving with her."

Of course it is. Jenna Anderson Regan blows into town from Youngstown, Ohio, and charms everyone in the county. I leave for what I think is a dream job and when it fails, the seniors have a field day.

"Do you think I'm a failure because I came back?" I brush my bangs out of my eye, a nervous habit I've had since at least the third grade.

Dad leans in and places his hand on my shoulder. "Absolutely not. You're going to find your place in life. You know how Shirley can be. That's just her way."

I stand, clutching my pillow. "Thanks. I know I was kind of a brat before. I thought all the answers to my life were in New York City. I acted as if these mountains were a prison."

"A lot of us who grew up here felt the same way. Leaving isn't bad, as long as you don't burn bridges. I couldn't have become a lawyer without leaving Speculator Falls for a while." Dad's smile exudes warmth and understanding. I never thought about him struggling with living in Speculator Falls.

Burn bridges. Like the flaming embers I left behind when I walked away from a building full of furious senior citizens. The boyfriend I didn't even have the courage to say goodbye to went on to marry a city girl who made the senior center thrive. I am a failure.

"And now you can be like Wayne. This area wasn't his first choice, but he's making it work."

With failures like me passing out on his watch, he'll do just fine.

⧗⧗⧗

Once Mom understands I don't have a concussion, she insists I sleep in and she'll also assert on opening the department store alone, but I can't let her. My head doesn't ache from the fall as much as from overthinking. Not long ago, I was waking up on the twelfth floor of a city apartment, preparing for work as an event planner. Working for my mom never entered my mind. And yet, here I am, pushing open the door to another October day void of customers.

"Trish. I told you I could manage for a few hours." Mom walks over and gives me a hug.

I offer a small smile. "I know. I couldn't sleep anymore, so, I thought I'd see if you need help."

She looks around. "Sara's senior exercise class came here earlier to look around. You could see if anything needs straightening up."

She bites her lip for a moment. "Actually, there is something. Your father asked if I could go to the library and do some research for him. I think it's council related, I never can keep up. Anyway, if you don't mind watching the store, I could do that." She walks behind the counter and picks up her purse.

"Sure. No problem. I'll straighten up, too."

"I know you will, Honey." She squeezes my arm on her way to the door. "I can't tell you how blessed I am to have you back."

I spend the next hour checking each rack to make sure clothes are hanging and in the right order. Turns out the seniors had a field day with the clearance rack, and things are even missing. Looks like they didn't just browse, but actually made some purchases.

"Trish? Are you here?"

A female's voice floats to my side of the store. In less than five seconds, Jenna Regan is in front of me.

"Oh, you are. I wanted to check on you. Shirley told me what happened. I was at JB's last night while Ben closed, so I ran over here and closed with her. I hope we did okay." Her voice sounds like pure sugar. I want to find something, anything wrong with her. But like the rest of Speculator Falls, I can't.

"My mom opened. She didn't say anything, so you must have done well. Thanks for helping. And checking on me. I'm fine." I keep re-arranging the clothes on the racks, although I already tidied them.

Jenna joins me. "Shirley gave me her version of the conversation. I've been around her long enough to know she can come on a bit strong."

My shoulders relax as we find common ground beyond Ben and the senior center. "She's no dainty flower, that's for sure."

"I'm sorry if she hurt your feelings or offended you."

I shrug and move to the glove table. "I'm not fragile, either. Which is good. I gather the seniors are still mad because I left the way I did."

Jenna sighs and rests her hands on her stomach. "They can carry a grudge. Makes me sad because we see most of them on Sundays at church."

"Well, I can't blame them. I thought only of myself and never considered the consequences. I didn't think Ben would close the building." I remember Mom telling me he had the council vote for that not long after I left. I'm sure it was his way of processing the pain I caused, especially when he was grieving the loss of his grandfather.

Jenna smiles. "It's in the past. It worked out for them, and I'd like to think it worked for Ben." She winks.

Oh, honestly. I can't be her BFF. It's like pickle juice and candy.

"Right. Well, I guess things will work out for me. I'll just give it time."

Jenna walks over and gives me a hug. "I'd like to help."

I step back. "How?"

"Let's show them you've changed. Because I know you have."

"Thanks. But, I'm not sure the seniors are as open-minded as you are."

"Let's create an event that features them, you, and the department store." She looks around, making a clicking sound as if she's deep in thought. After a few quiet moments, she snaps her fingers. "Let's have a senior fashion show. You're an event planner, right? Well, plan an event with me. Let the seniors be your models. And convince your mom to let them wear Speculator Department Store clothes."

☃☃☃

By the time Mom returns mid-afternoon, I'm actually excited to share Jenna's idea. "Just to be clear, my motivation isn't to make the senior center members like me. Truth is, I love the idea of planning something that could help draw some business to the store."

Mom walks over and gives me a tight hug. As an only child, I never lacked physical affection. "Trish, I love it. I'm actually embarrassed I never thought of such a thing."

"I know, I didn't either. And I used to be the senior center director."

We gather at the register where she takes out a notebook.

"Retail always works a season ahead, so if we plan to do this soon, we can have a winter fashion show. My shipment is coming in this week."

I reach for a pencil. "Do you think we could offer a discount to the models and a smaller discount to anyone who attends that day?"

Mom looks up from the notebook with a wide smile. "Great idea. Do you know Jenna's schedule? Could you call her and set up a meeting at Jack Frosty's this week? The shipment comes Wednesday, so maybe Thursday or Friday."

I take in a deep breath and exhale. "Of course." I need to get excited about working with Ben's wife. It's not her that's the problem. It's me.

Mom pushes the notebook aside and reaches for my hand. "You're doing an excellent job at the store. The plans you have are amazing. That's a confirmation to me."

I swipe at my bangs again. "I'm happy to help. You know that."

"I do. But there's more." She squeezes my hand.

"O...kay. Are you sick? Is Daddy?" I pull my hand away.

"No. We're healthy as can be. It's about the store. Your father and I talked about it last night as we drove back from Albany. He'd like to retire in about eighteen months."

"Wow. That's not long."

"It's not. He has a lot of work to wrap up and prepare for the next person. He's been mentoring a lawyer from Syracuse who is looking for his own business. He's considering buying the firm from your father."

This shouldn't surprise me, but the more she speaks, the more my stomach churns. "You guys have been planning. But I don't understand. What does that have to do with the store?" I search my mom's kind eyes.

"I took over the store once you were in high school. But before we had you, I was a paralegal. Your dad has a lot of work, and he could use my help."

"Are you going to close the store early so you can go to Daddy's office and help out?"

She chuckled and shook her head. "No, Sweetheart. I'm going to have you run the store. And that frees me up to work with your dad."

⧗⧗⧗

Before I can process what Mom shared, she's out the door and headed to Dad's office. If she's letting me run the store, then I have a funny feeling that means the fashion show is going to be up to me and Jenna. The sooner I set something up with her, the better.

JB's grocery store is across the street from the Speculator Falls Department Store. The contrast between my NYC life and Speculator Falls is laughable. The village has one stop sign and that's at the intersection between Ben's store and mom's. Mine. Whatever. I take a chance on Jenna being there as Ben closes, knowing the senior center is already locked up.

A teen greets me as the automatic doors swing open. He's sweeping near the newspaper racks. "Hey." He looks to the back where Ben's office is. "I mean, welcome."

"Good evening. Noah?" I remember hearing that Carla Marshall and Wayne's son helps out after school.

"Yeah. I mean, yes. That's me. Ben has me working on customer service and my manners." Noah rolls his brown eyes.

Sounds like the Speculator Falls businessman of the year, three years running. "It's smart to learn."

"Can I help you with something? There are some half-moon cookies left."

"No, not today. I wondered if Jenna was here. Mrs. Regan." I almost wince saying it. Not that long ago, Ben fantasized about that being my name.

He turns to the back. "I saw her earlier. Maybe she's in

restroom?"

I'm not that desperate to see her. "I can wait."

He nods and returns to sweeping while I saunter over to the middle aisles where the local authors' books rest. I open a mystery as the automatic doors open.

"Hey, Dad." Noah stops his task.

Dad? As in, Wayne Peterson, Dad?

I toss the book and start back to the front.

"Noah. I thought I'd find you here. I wanted to check with you about the weekend. There's a 10k in Indian Lake. Wanna run with the old man?"

I stop near the clearance bakery items, picking up the half-moon cookies and inspecting them. Every few seconds I steal a peek at Wayne, wearing a blue check flannel shirt.

"With you? Don't you mean blow past you?" Noah elbows his dad.

And then I giggle.

Wayne steps to the side. "Trish?"

I put down the cookies. "Oh, sorry. I didn't mean to eavesdrop. Noah just made me laugh." I stick a few strands of hair behind my ear.

Wayne lets out a low chuckle that sends shivers down my back. "He thinks he's funny."

"Come on, Dad. You know I'm a better runner than you."

Wayne throws his hands up in mock surrender. "Okay, I'll give you that. And you probably get that from your mom, anyway. But what do you think? Wanna go?" He gives Noah a light punch in the forearm, then turns to me. "Trish, do you run? If you're feeling better you could join us."

Noah nods. "Dad's right. If you run, you should come with."

I remember seeing Carla run all over town before she married Will Marshall. There's no way I can run like her. But with Wayne's gorgeous eyes and growing beard tempting me, I'm going to try.

"I'd love to. You'll go easy on me, right?" I wink.

# Chapter Three

Mom decides mornings will be training time for me to take over the store. I already know Will Marshall is our delivery driver, but she shows me purchase orders and merchandiser information. Computer programs that display what items moved quickly, what didn't, how long before she put things on clearance. As she clicks away I realize she's done an outstanding job with very little help.

I put my hands on my hips and face her. "Are you sure about this?"

"About what?"

"Leaving the day-to-day operations to me. You've done a fantastic job. I don't want to mess it up." I play with my hair as I watch her switch screens.

"I doubt you'll mess it up. You went to school for things like this. You've worked in New York City. I think you can handle the only department store in Speculator Falls."

In her office she has filing cabinets and magazines. Everything has a place.

"Do you have plans to bring anyone else in?" I twist my hair around my index finger.

"Trish, that's for you to decide. With the holidays coming up, it's not a bad idea. But sweetheart, I'm trusting you with everything here."

My finger turns color, so I unwind the strands and return my focus to the monitor. It hits me as I look at the merchandise history.

Everything has a place but me.

⧗⧗⧗

Not long after Mom leaves to help Dad for the afternoon, Jenna enters the store. Her senior center director schedule used to be mine, so I know she's taking her lunch break.

She joins me at the register and leans on the counter. "Oh, good. You're here. I heard you stopped by yesterday. Sorry we didn't connect."

"No problem. I wanted to let you know my Mom loved the fashion show idea with the senior center. She thought if we want to do a holiday themed show, we should start planning immediately."

Jenna puts her purse on the counter and pulls out a notebook and pen. "I agree. She's probably getting the winter shipment anytime, right?"

A sigh escapes. "Actually, I'm getting the shipment. Mom announced that she's handing the store management over to me while she helps Dad. I guess this fashion show is between you and me." I glance her way, but she has no reaction.

"Well, I don't know what you think, but I'm excited. For both things. You'll be great here, and I know the fashion show will be an amazing success for the store, too." As awful as I was to her when I first got back to town, she never brings it up. A wave of guilt for the way I treated her sweeps over me.

"Thanks, Jenna. Your encouragement means a lot, and I definitely need your help. So, want to get started planning?"

"Absolutely. Let me call Shirley and tell her that I'm in a meeting so she won't worry." She tugs on her purse until her phone spills out.

Shirley? The woman who still carries a grudge because I left Speculator Falls, loves Jenna so much she keeps tabs on her?

I refuse to be jealous. But it's going to take extra prayer time to get there.

An hour later, Jenna closes her notebook and smiles. "I think we have a great start. Once you get the shipment in and on display I'll bring some of the seniors over and we'll pick out some clothes. I love the idea of making the show part of the center's Christmas party. We'll have a full house. It will be so much fun."

Her enthusiasm is contagious as I reach for a pad and pencil and scribble notes. "I'll print out tickets so that each center member and guest receives an invitation to a VIP shopping event that includes their discount. I'll open the store early one morning just for them so they can do some Christmas shopping. Maybe even change the front window display to promote both the fashion show and the VIP event." The more I talk, the more excited I am.

Jenna breaks out in a mischievous smile. "That's fantastic. Now, I have one more idea I want you to think about."

I raise my eyebrows. "Why do I think I'm not going to like this?"

She rolls her eyes as the front door chimes and Carla Marshall walks in. "You will. In time. I want you to emcee the fashion show." Jenna winks.

Carla grins as soon as she sees her best friend and joins her at the counter.

Jenna steps aside to make room for her friend to stand with us. "Hey, Carla. Trish and I are planning a fashion show at the center featuring clothes from here. Isn't that a great idea?"

"It is. Why didn't you guys think of it before?" She looks to both of us and then giggles.

I clear my throat and focus on my pencil. "Good point. Jenna thinks I should emcee it, but let's be honest. The seniors don't like me. I gave them good reason, but still."

Jenna shakes her head. "That's exactly why I think you should do it. Let's show them you've changed and you're where God wants you to be. And, they love coupons. They'll forgive you once you tell them about their VIP shopping experience."

Carla nods. "True. Will says he's seen a couple seniors get physical trying to beat the other to the coupons in the Sunday paper."

I raise my hands in surrender. "Okay. I'll do it. Thanks, Jenna. I think you're going to have a great Christmas party. Now, Carla, is there something I can help you with?"

Now it's her turn to clear her throat. "Sorry. I'm here to see Jenna." She turns to her friend. "Will was at the center for lunch and said you were here. You left a message that you had something to tell me?"

The two face me, and I suddenly feel like the last girl left in gym class that neither team wants for kickball.

Jenna takes a deep breath and brings her hands to her face, covering everything but her eyes for a moment. "I do." She places her hands on the counter.

I step back. "I can go in the next room and give you privacy."

It's quiet for a moment, and then Jenna shakes her head. "No. It's okay. The only people that know are Ben, my family, Sara, and Shirley, because she heard me in the restroom."

Carla gasps. "You're pregnant."

Jenna squeals and reaches for Carla. "I am. I want to tell the whole world but we want to wait until the first trimester is over. And, Ben has a point. As soon as the seniors find out, I'm not going to get a second to myself. They worry about me as it is. The pregnancy will take their overprotectiveness to extremes."

I smile, although I can feel a pit forming in my stomach. Jenna and Ben deserve all their happy news. But, I remember when it was us in high school talking about the future. "Congratulations. You guys will be amazing parents."

"Trish is right. I'm so excited for you." Carla hugs her.

Jenna steps back, but then bites her lip and returns to the counter. "Enough about me. Trish has news, too."

I look to Jenna. "I do?"

"The store? Your mom?" She nudges me.

I nod and start to speak, but the door chime sounds and in comes Wayne. I smile, excited to see that toned paramedic with ocean eyes, and then remember his history with Carla.

"Hey, Trish. I was just checking to see if you were still feeling...oh. I didn't see you had customers. Jenna. Carla." He smiles, but looks down as he says Noah's mom's name.

Jenna glances at Carla, but she doesn't appear bothered with Wayne's presence.

"It's okay. I've got to get home and start dinner." She turns to Jenna. "Girl, I'll be in touch." She waves and starts for the door.

Jenna sees that Wayne isn't moving, so she zips up her coat.

"Right. I need to get back to the center or Shirley will put out an APB on me. Good to see you, Wayne. Thanks, Trish." She winks at me as she leaves.

Wayne wastes no time moving to the counter where Jenna had just been. "I hope I didn't scare them away. I wanted to see how you were doing and make sure you were up to the run later this week."

I face him and see the chin stubble. It's hard not to stare. "No, Jenna and I finished a meeting, and Carla was looking for her. It's okay." I force myself to look elsewhere. "I'm feeling well. I admit I'm nervous about running with two pros like you and Noah, but I'm looking forward to it."

He chuckles, another sound that is as sweet as the German chocolate cake I had for dessert last night. "I think professional is pretty generous. I try to get in a run around my house after work, but I haven't been in a race in a while. Noah ran track last year and did well. He'll be the one to beat."

The door sings again and I remember this is a store and I'm on the clock. It can't all be social time. Then I realize the customer is business mogul Kyle Swarthmore, a guy I dated back when Ben and I took a break before our true end.

Kyle sidles up next to Wayne.

"Good afternoon. Trish, I'm surprised to see you here. Rumor has it that older woman from the senior center, Shirley, intimidated you so harshly the other day that you passed out."

Wayne's gaze on Kyle narrows.

"You shouldn't believe everything you hear, Kyle. After all, I heard you were a decent businessman." I cross my arms and give a "so there" look.

Kyle laughs. "Very funny, Trish. I wish you'd been this entertaining when we were dating. And I use that term loosely for what happened between us."

The feeling in my stomach now feels like a boulder trying to move to my throat.

I look to Wayne and notice he clenches his fist, but stays silent.

"Kyle, do you need something?"

He unbuttons his long, wool coat. "I have an important business meeting first thing in Albany and need a good tie to go with my power suit. Nothing is open that early in the city, so I wondered if your store might have something."

I look to Wayne and shrug as I leave the register area and point Kyle to the ties.

"Everything is on this table. Let me know if you need anything else." I walk back to Wayne.

Wayne keeps his eye on Kyle as he leans in closer to me. "You, you were with that jerk?"

## Chapter Four

I can't believe I'm ready to leave the house for a race barely after sunrise. With a few minutes to spare before Wayne's due to pick me up, it's tempting to spend time on my hair to impress him. I can't forget the image of him standing over me after my fainting spell. My goal is to make a wonderful memory for him about something, anything, today.

Even as a newbie runner I know to put my hair in a ponytail. He definitely isn't going to compliment my fitness skills. By the time he pulls up in the health care clinic SUV, my confidence level for the day has gone back to bed.

He puts the vehicle in park, runs around to the passenger side, and opens the door.

"Hey, Trish. Ready for a great run for charity?" He smiles, his breath visible in the frosty air.

I climb in, realizing Noah is in the middle.

The teen offers a limp wave. "Hi. Dad gets to use the company vehicle." Noah rolls his eyes.

Wayne switches gears and starts for Indian Lake. "Sorry about that. I'm backup for today. There are two EMTs on call, but if it's serious, I'll get paged."

Noah looks to me. If the teen can read minds, then he knows I'm wondering if the medical attention will be for me.

☒☒☒

An hour later, we're registered and ready to start. The men are stretching, so I follow suit. I haven't been to Indian Lake in years, and knowing my bratty old self, I probably kicked and screamed the whole way. Now I'm looking at store fronts, shocked by the growth of business in the area. It's so much more than the basic gas station and post office. A quick glance reveals there's a hardware store. Insurance office. Chamber of Commerce. Restaurant. Bakery. Gas station. And the potential to promote the stores and their space.

"Trish? You okay?" Wayne touches my shoulder, not only

sending a chill up my spine, but bringing me back to reality.

Please don't let my smile look as giddy as I feel. "What? Oh, sorry. I can't believe how much this area has expanded. I guess it's been awhile since I've been here."

"So, you weren't thinking about that Kyle guy?" Wayne's eyes seem to pierce through mine, a gaze penetrating enough to leave a lump in my throat.

My reaction is about the same as if a mosquito darted into my mouth. "Swarthmore? No. That would be a nightmare." My history with the New Jersey businessman was brief, but brutal.

Wayne lifts his hand and reaches down to tie his shoe. "Can I ask, what made you date that jerk, anyway?"

Noah folds his arms and taps his foot, as if he's waiting for me to share, too.

I open my mouth, then close it. A few times. Finding the words isn't easy. "I'd like to think I'm not the same person I was back then. I was selfish. Ben and I were off-again and I was angry at a lot of things. I didn't like my job at the senior center. I felt stuck in Speculator Falls. My parents are successful, beloved people and I wasn't. Kyle seemed like a good rebellious choice for me at the time. I was wrong."

Noah smirks. "Yeah, you were."

An announcer informs us that the race will begin in ten minutes, and I'm thankful for the distraction. My coffee starts to kick in, so I look for a portable bathroom. "I'll be back. Need a girl's room."

Noah glances at Wayne, and his eyes seem to expand as I make my little announcement. What? Am I the only one that needs a bathroom after three cups of coffee?

⧗⧗⧗

Once back from the port-a-potty, everyone is lined up and waiting for the signal to start. Swarms of people with sweatbands, gadgets that look like they monitor steps and heartrates, and running shoes that appear to cost more than my car fill the starting area.

They're stretching, chatting with each other, and working on breathing exercises. These folks look like they run these events often. And then there's me.

Wayne reaches for my elbow, and pulls me aside. His eyes close, and he prays.

"Father, I ask You to keep us strong to run this race, and healthy to run this race. Thank You that Trish is here with us. Whether we make the 5k or the 10, all thanks goes to You. Amen."

You mean there's a choice on how much to run? Cuz if I hit the bare minimum, it's going to be a flat-out miracle.

With the crack of gunshot and the temptation to duck, thanks to my months in the city, the race's start isn't so bad. The three of us have a decent pace going. Those guys are holding back. There's no way I should be keeping up with them.

After the first mile, I look over and see Noah has earbuds in and he's in some kind of zone. The kid looks like a natural runner. Each of my steps is fueled by thoughts. How weird is it that I'm running next to a guy my age who has a teenaged son? How odd that the paramedic I knew in passing is now a friend. If he wants more, that's okay with me.

And as that line of thinking ran a marathon of its own, my stomach decided to seize into a vise-like grip. The cramp was so strong that I went from a good rhythm to a complete stop.

"Oh boy." I hold my abdomen as the two notice my absence and race back.

"What's wrong?" Noah pulls out the earbuds.

I double over. "I'm not sure. Cramps. Ow. Wow."

Wayne puts his hand on my back, but talks to his son. "Go on ahead. She'll be okay. I think her coffee is punishing her."

Noah's voice changes like a typical teenaged boy. "Can I do the full 10k?"

Wayne's voice is calm and steady, the complete opposite of how my stomach feels. "Sure, Noah. We'll find you. Keep your phone on."

Still hunched over, I hear pounding feet on pavement, an even rhythm that fades with each step. Noah's departure leaves Wayne and me alone. With his warm touch on my back.

His soothing voice is like butter on hot pancakes. "Let's head to the side of the road so we don't get mowed down by the others."

Each step produces a guttural moan I didn't even know I could make.

His hand remains on the middle of my back and he bends down so our faces are inches apart. "Explain the pain to me, Trish."

Thanks to heavy breathing, I sound like a prank phone caller when I speak. "Like my intestines are twisted into a limp dishrag."

He sighs. "Okay, listen. It sounds like your pre-race routine wasn't very..." Wayne's going to call me out for not being a real athlete. My stomach seizes again. "Kind to you. Usually runners drink, but not cups of coffee. More like sips. We eat a light breakfast, but not right before, and not with a drink. C'mon, we're going to keep moving, but walk. If you feel up to it, we'll pick up the pace later. If not, that's okay. I'm sorry, I assumed you ran a race before." He winks, and the smoldering gaze feels like a miracle cure. I don't feel as stupid, and the cramps don't feel as awful. But still, I'm busted. Wayne knows I'm not a runner.

A group of about a dozen runners pass us. "What about you? You should catch up to Noah."

He waves me off. "Don't worry about him. A few of his friends from school are here. I'm sure he's grateful to be on his own so he can find them. His pace is much faster than he was letting on, he's off and running."

More racers breeze past. "Okay. If you say so." And as soon as I utter the word, "so," from the pit of my belly comes a belch so loud the group that just glided by turns around to find the culprit.

⧖⧖⧖

I've never been so glad to end an event, and to have a gorgeous man at my side as a bonus. My cheeks have hopefully returned to their pale color after my mortifying burp in Wayne's face. We finish the 3.1 mile run and find the refreshment tent.

Wayne smiles and reaches for a bottle, handing it to me. "I expect Noah to show up soon. Help yourself. Water might help your stomach."

I nod, still too petrified to speak.

Wayne seems to recognize someone as he waves and gestures them over. They are in the same type of uniform Wayne wore the day I fainted, so I suspect it's the EMTs on duty.

"Hey, Peterson. Too tired to do the full race?" The man who looks a little younger than us but older than Noah gives Wayne a jab in the arm.

Wayne chuckles. "Something like that. Say, this is Trish Maxwell. Trish, this is Brad Wagner and Jill Bryant."

Brad's eyes widen as he shakes my hand and glances at Wayne. Wish I could read minds, but my reaction is the same when Jill steps out from behind Brad. She's a petite thing who makes the uniform look so fashionable I almost want to order it for the store.

Jill extends a hand. "Hi. Nice to meet you. Trish Maxwell. The name is familiar." She looks like she's thinking hard, and I really want to say something sarcastic, but that's the old Trish.

Brad snaps his fingers. "Are you a model? Cuz your legs look like they know a runway."

Blech. Forget the runway. This guy makes me want to run away.

Jill shakes her head. "No, that's not it. Oh, I remember! You were a patient at the health center. I saw your name in Wayne's paperwork. Single, white female who passed out. Suspected anxiety attack." She smiles the more she realizes she's got it figured out.

Wayne's demeanor seems to change. His gaze narrows and he lowers his voice. "Jill, you can't discuss our work like that. You're violating healthcare confidentiality."

Jill's smile disappears and she keeps her attention on me. "Sorry.

Engaged

I was talking about you, so, no harm, right, Tish?"

I clear my throat. "It's Trish."

☧☧☧

When Noah announces an hour and a half later that he needs to get back to his mom's, I want to hug him. The day's been nothing short of a disaster and I want to bury myself in Oreos and ice cream. The only thing that brings solace is thinking about the Indian Lake storefronts. So many store-decorating themes race through my mind that I wish my race had been as fruitful.

"You're kind of quiet over there." Wayne sneaks a peek my way before returning his eyes to the road.

"I'm thinking."

Wayne wastes no time guessing. "About the burp? It was the cramps talking."

My smile is tight. "No, I'd like to erase that from my mind."

Noah takes a turn. "Was it doubling over during the race and having to stop?"

Wayne slows down as he approaches yet another curve on Route 30. "Noah, how about we let Trish explain."

My pace picks up the more I share. "It's kind of work related. I noticed the growth around Indian Lake since the last time I was here. I bet they get decent traffic, but the store fronts don't showcase the merchandise. Then that reminded me of the department store. I have some ideas for the window front there, especially with the fashion show we're doing with the senior center."

Noah nods. "Interesting. I never would have thought about that, but it's true. Sometimes it's what I see in the window that makes me and my friends go inside."

I grin. "Exactly. That's what I want to capitalize on to help out my mom."

Wayne shares a dazzling smile. "You have a lot of creativity, Trish. This area definitely needs your expertise."

My smile fades. "Oh. I can help dress up the store, but that's it. I mean, I have to work on my future and find a permanent job."

Noah's voice cracks again. "In Speculator Falls, right?"

Silence fills the vehicle. Returning to my hometown was a place to heal from my job rejection simply because I was the last hired and funds weren't there to keep me. I still love what I did in New York. Events planning. Watching executives toast a glass of champagne because they have new business thanks to my hard work. The storefronts here in the mountains? I want to help my mom and her store. Not all of the Adirondack Mountain businesses.

Wayne looks over to me. "You okay?"

My sigh speaks volumes. "Yes. No. I don't know."

# Engaged

# Chapter Five

Fifteen minutes later, and a lot of hard work changing the subject to avoid the New York question, we're pulling into the Marshall driveway. The long day drags on as I picture Carla coming out to greet us. We had a decent chat at the department store with Jenna, but how about now? Will she realize I have a crush on her son's father? Will she care?

Although barely dusk, a porch light comes on as Wayne puts the SUV in park. The front door opens and Carla steps out.

I open the door and slide out so Noah can exit.

"Hope your stomach's better." He's not doing well hiding his smirk.

It's hard not to laugh. What the teen saw today had to be memorable. Cramps. Burps. "Thanks." With my one foot in the passenger seat, Carla's greeting stops me.

"Hi, Trish. Wayne. How was the race?"

I turn around and stand next to her, looking for sarcasm, anger, anything that would tell me to back away from Wayne and her son. "The guys did fantastic. Noah's a natural. I think I need to hang up my running shoes." My laughter sounds forced.

She glances at Wayne, then pats her boy on the back. "This one outruns me every time. I'm sure you'll get the hang of it, Trish." She looks again to Wayne, and when she speaks to him, I can't help but notice the growing lump in my throat. "Thanks for bringing him home."

He nods, and Noah waves. "See ya Wednesday, Dad." With that, the teen jogs into the house, his mom at his side. I can only imagine how he'll recap the day between my cramps, burps, and meeting Brad and Jill, the obnoxious paramedics.

Once I'm buckled in, Wayne doesn't make a move to put the car in gear. "Are you in a hurry to be home?"

With Noah gone, it feels like there is a lot of room up front.

My heartrate accelerates. "Not really. Why?"

"I could eat. Want to go to Jack Frosty's?"
*With the handsome paramedic? Sure thing.*

⧗ ⧗ ⧗

Thankfully, we find a booth without trouble. Wendy Simmons, the manager, locks eyes with me and waves, her blond ponytail bounces as she moves. There's still enough time for Wayne and me to enjoy a quick bite before Jack Frosty's closes.

Wayne hands me a menu and I stifle a laugh. Every teen who grows up here endures a rite of passage, working at Frosty's at least one summer. I know the menu thanks to working here all through high school. Our fingers touch as I take the laminated folder, and I'm glad to have something to hold onto.

He peruses the menu for a minute, nods, and places it on the table. His eyes meet mine, and I can barely swallow. He is so handsome, I almost miss his question. "I'm curious. You talked a little about how you used to be, and I admit, I've heard a little about you over the short time I've lived here, yet I can't say what I've heard and seen matches up."

I'd like to use my menu as a standing wall to hide my face. "I'm not proud of who I was, and I'm ashamed it wasn't that long ago. It's easy to guess what you heard. Trish Maxwell, thinks she's too important for Speculator Falls. Trish, the girl that broke Ben's heart. Then there's the one about how I deserved dating and getting dumped by Kyle Swarthmore." My voice rises as my cheeks burn. "Oh, I'm sure you heard I'm a selfish ice princess who left the senior center members in the cold by leaving for New York City without warning. And lastly, Trish, the brat who got what she had coming to her when the big job was a bust and she had to come back to the mountains she used to make fun of."

Wayne lets out a whistle. "Wow. Kind of hard on yourself, don't you think?"

Wendy steps behind the counter and peeks at us before finishing up filling a drink order. This is probably the most excitement she's seen all day.

"Be honest, Wayne, what I repeated just now is what you heard. And, the people that said those things weren't wrong."

He keeps his focus on me. "What made you hate it here?"

I start folding my napkin. "I think I had a grass-is-greener complex. I'd watch Big Apple based movies from JB's, and it all seemed so glamourous. I was lonely as an only child, and I didn't have a lot of friends in school."

With drinks on the table, he opens the straw paper and inserts a straw in my drink. "Do you think it's because you're so stunning?"

I raise my eyebrows. Is he serious? "You're kind, but that's the last thing on my mind. I think it's because I was mean. Even as an adult with my dream job, I kept acting spoiled thinking that was part of the corporate world. Maybe it's true. But whatever the case, I was a small fish in a gigantic ocean. Many times my co-workers mocked my ideas for being too small. When the budget needed tightening, it wasn't hard for them to let me go." I hit the ice with the straw, not daring to look at him.

I sense he's keeping his gaze on me, and it's exhilarating and frightening. "Sounds like a rough time."

"When I came back, I felt like a failure. Seeing a city girl like Jenna move here and so effortlessly blend in, not to mention make Ben forget he ever had a broken heart, that was hard to take. I wasn't nice to her. After a while it hit me, I had no job. No prospects. And it broke me. I kind of went into a depression, mad at my failure, clueless about my future. I've been floundering ever since."

Wendy returns for our orders, and its perfect timing. So much hasn't changed in my life, and I hate revisiting it all. Even if a handsome man is asking to hear my story.

After we give our order, Wayne sighs. "I think it's all about perspective. What seems like punishment to you, for me is opportunity."

Okay, color me confused. "I need some explanation on that one. It sounds to me like you're trying to make me feel better."

Wayne reaches across the table and gives my hand a quick squeeze. My napkin squishes between us. "Trish, you're too hard on yourself."

If all the ice in my glass melts with the heat in his touch, I wouldn't be surprised.

"Okay, look at it this way. Maybe God's plan was to show you how to appreciate what you had all along. That this is a great place to live with nice people. And moving back, it wasn't as a failure, but to provide vision for a village that needs the gifts you have."

"Like?" I lean on my hands and keep my eyes on his.

"What you were saying earlier. You have ideas to increase business by creating great storefronts. Your mom already believes in you to manage the department store. And you can't be too hated if Jenna wants to partner with you for an event with the seniors that you claim don't care for you."

Wayne missed his calling. The only other person who can spin like that is my dad. The lawyer.

"Thank you. You're very kind. Either way, that's my story."

We sit in silence for a while, before I remember something he said.

"Okay, a question for you." I grin.

He spreads his arms wide. "I'm an open book. Go for it."

"What do you mean stunning? In less than a week you've rescued me from a fainting spell and cramps. Nothing beautiful about that."

Wayne lets out a hearty laugh. "See, we're back to perspective. I've enjoyed everything about meeting and getting to know you better."

I roll my eyes. "You didn't answer me."

"Fair enough. Have you looked in a mirror? You belong on a magazine cover without needing airbrushing. C'mon. Long blonde hair with crystal blue eyes. I can see how all of Speculator Falls saw you and Ben as the couple of the decade when you were in high school. You two look like movie stars. Same for why Kyle honed in on you. You were something he wanted to own."

"You think I'm a Barbie doll?" I wish the menus were still on the table so I could mask my hurt.

"No, Trish. Not at all. You're a beautiful woman who is intelligent to boot. Now everyone is getting to see the warmth you have, too. That's a stunning package if you ask me. Speaking of questions, I have one more."

Lord, please have the waitress deliver our food. Right now.

Wayne's smile is full of warmth. "You don't have to answer if you don't want to."

"All right. Go ahead."

"If a job comes up that isn't based around here, say, back in New York, would you take it?"

Before I can reply, Wendy arrives with our plates. And I want to hug her.

He places his napkin on his lap and once she leaves, he asks, "Do you mind if I say grace?"

I shake my head. That's twice today he's prayed aloud.

"Father, thank You for this day and all that came with it. Bless our time together, our conversation, the food, and the hands that prepared it. In Christ's name, Amen."

"Amen." I open my eyes and reach for a fry. "Can I ask more questions?"

"Absolutely. Don't mind me, I'm going to chow down on this burger, though."

I swallow my food. "I've heard a little about you as well. When did you become religious?"

Whether it's my question or the burger, he starts to cough. He takes a few sips of water and recovers. "Food went down the wrong pipe. That's a great question, and I could answer it in one word. Noah."

"You want to be a good dad and set an example?"

He shakes his head. "That makes sense, but no. He was raised in the church and has a good head on his shoulders. His faith is real. He kept inviting me to church after I moved here and sometimes I'd show, but my motives weren't pure. For a time I was hoping to woo Carla back."

I almost drop my fork.

"Noah got in a little trouble at school and Carla chose Will, which by the way, was the best choice for everyone. Noah invited me to church, and there was something in his eyes. It was more than sitting with him or chatting after service in the sanctuary. He needed to see his dad have a relationship with Christ. Pastor Reynolds gave a great message on the topic of real faith versus being a poser, and I surrendered it all."

With my fries gone, it's my turn to talk. "That's incredible. I confess, I'm not there yet. I've always attended and appreciated the messages. For a long time it was what was expected of me, so I never took faith seriously."

"I don't think I would have without Noah. I became a parent in an irresponsible way, and I stayed immature for a long time. Carla has every right to say horrible things about me, but she's extended such grace. But if you went to our hometown, you'd hear a lot of bad things about me."

I sip my water. "We're quite the pair."

As soon as the words leave my mouth, I want to crawl under the table. Wayne's chuckle is sweet and disarms my panic. "I agree. It's been great spending the day with you. One more question, if you're up for it."

*Do I want pie? Will I run another race with him? Is marriage on the table? What?*

"I'm ready."

He slides both hands over to my side of the table and reaches for my trembling hands. "Do you want to do this again sometime? Soon?"

Engaged

# Chapter Six

With my hair in a messy bun and a colored pencil anchored in my mouth, I look at my sketch pad. Rough drawings of Speculator Falls storefronts fill the pages. My laptop's open to Google and several tabs with other Adirondack villages and their merchants.

A soft knock disrupts my research as Dad nudges my bedroom door. "You okay? It's your day off and I haven't seen much of you."

I drop the pencil from my mouth and wave him in, making room for him to sit on my canopy bed. "Come, in, I want to show you something."

He saunters in, ducking under the frilly material before taking a seat. His earthy-smelling cologne trails after him, a scent I remember from childhood. "Sketching? I haven't seen you do that in a long time."

I leaf through the different pages and decide to show him the senior center window design advertising the fashion show. "When I went to Indian Lake I was surprised by how much the village has changed. It offers a lot more shopping and business opportunities, but it didn't look like they were capitalizing on it. I started thinking about window appeal. Decorating the windows and the front displays to attract more people, and hopefully, business for them."

He lifts the book up to the light, nods, and thumbs through other pages. "You've sketched more than Speculator Falls here. This is Gloversville." He flips another paper. "Wow. Even Lake Placid."

Okay, so my vision covers a lot of territory. After all, the Adirondacks have over a million acres. "What do you think?"

"Very professional. You customized each design. So, what's going on? Hobby? New direction for you?" Dad pauses from looking at the sketches and raises his eyebrows while turning toward me.

"I, um, I'm not sure. I thought I was helping mom at the store without any real commitment, but she's gone a lot, which I understand. You need the help. I also peek at job postings back in the city." I push the laptop monitor back to reveal all the searches.

"But this, I haven't felt excited about something for a long time. I thought I'd start with asking Jenna if I can dress the senior center front for the fashion show. If that goes well, who knows?"

He pats my knee before standing. "God knows, honey. Have you prayed about it?"

Oh, right. That. "I will."

"Good. I know things haven't gone exactly how you thought they would the last couple years. But the verse I use for everything as a husband, father, lawyer, everything, is true. 'Trust the Lord with all your heart and lean not on your own understanding; in all your ways submit to him, and he will make your paths straight.' God's never failed me. Not once." He winks.

"I know." But I've failed Him. "You have an amazing life, and you deserve it."

He walks to the door. "All God's doing. I promise, you put your trust in Him, and your life will be amazing, too. Not easy, but blessed. Your mom's at the store and is closing tonight, so it's just us. How about I order a pizza for dinner?"

I gaze down and see the Four Corners Pizzeria sketch. "That I don't have to pray about. Sounds good."

⧗⧗⧗

Before going into work the next day, I bring my sketch pad to the senior center. Pulling into the gravel lot transports me back in time. Back when Ben and I were a couple, most everyone in town expected us to get engaged. I was the director, so restless and ready for change. Now, my stomach churns as I face the people I disappointed.

A noise that sounds like a door slam grabs my attention. "Trish? Is that you?"

I turn and see retired banker and Councilman Fred Beebe walking toward me. His white hair makes him look debonair, coupled with the deep blue cable knit sweater he's wearing. "It is. I'm hoping to meet with Jenna for a couple minutes before I head to the department store."

He nods and offers a warm smile as he steps ahead in order to open the front door for me. "Sounds interesting. New project?"

"I hope so. If Jenna agrees, I'd like to use the senior center as my experiment. If all goes well, maybe I can expand and make it a career." Talking to Fred comes naturally and I hope Jenna is as easy to pitch my idea to.

Once I duck past him, he follows me inside. "Something tells me whatever you're planning, you'll make it a success."

Before I can respond, Shirley clears her throat and holds up a clipboard. "Visitors need to sign in."

Fred chuckles. "We know the drill. Is Jenna here?"

She pushes her enormous glasses up the bridge of her nose. "Who wants to know?"

It's my turn to clear my throat so I can find my voice. "Me. I don't have an appointment, but if she has ten minutes, I'd like to talk with her."

Shirley leans to the right and looks past me, probably into Jenna's office. She picks up the phone and punches in three numbers. "Jenna, its Shirley. Trish Maxwell is here. She would like to talk to you, but doesn't have an appointment."

I look to Fred, who signs in. Only Shirley would phone Jenna when she could just as easily call out to her.

"Are you sure? Okay, you're the boss. Thanks. Bye." Shirley puts the ancient phone back in the cradle and focuses her beady eyes on me. "She has a busy schedule but said to come in."

Phew. I grip my sketch notebook and take a breath. "Thank you, Shirley." My voice shakes, but I refuse to let the volunteer secretary know she rattles me. I straighten my posture and lift my chin and I move toward my former office.

Jenna stands as soon as she sees me. Her smile is as bright as the halo I imagine she wears to bed at night. As much as I tried to find something wrong with her, I can't. It's no surprise everyone in town loves her. "Trish, what a surprise. What brings you by?" She gestures for me to take a seat.

"A favor. When I was in Indian Lake, I noticed how the businesses have changed over the years. I think there is potential across the Adirondacks to bring attention to the merchants." I pause, noticing she has her arms on her desk and focuses her attention on me.

"Interesting. How so?"

I open my book to my senior center sketch. "I'd like to explore the idea of creating visuals for the store fronts to bring attention to each business. I would custom design and create each one, and I wondered if I could start here. Use the fashion show as a backdrop to decorate your bay windows up front. If people enjoy it and you notice an increase in interest, I'd use the center as my exhibit to ask other businesses if I can do the same for them. My basic vision has me designing all of Speculator Falls."

"What's your long-term vision?" She holds her gaze without revealing her thoughts.

"If it's meant to be, I'd love to be a business that does this for all Adirondack merchants."

She bites her lip for a moment. "Where does finding another job in New York City fit in?"

Her question feels like a slap, but given my history, it's legitimate. "Honestly? I don't know. I'm excited about this idea. I'm helping my mom at the store, and I feel like I'm at a crossroads. But, I promise, I don't intend to leave town like before. What do you think?" Swallowing hard, I'd love to see Jenna blink. Laugh. Something.

She brings the sketch closer and flips through the others. After a couple minutes, she looks up and her smile is wide. "Trish, these are beautiful. I really think you have something here. I'd love for you to start here with the senior center. Make a supply list and I'll see if we have everything. Start as soon as you want. I'll even submit pictures to the paper so you get publicity."

The urge to jump up and hug her is overwhelming, but I stand and offer my hand. "I won't let you down. Also, let me know when your volunteer models want to come in to choose their clothes for the show. The entire process is going to be amazing. Thanks, Jenna."

She stands and takes a few steps toward the office door when her phone beeps. I peek out to the reception area and see Shirley waving at Jenna. She picks up the phone. As she listens, I can hear what Shirley is saying just from her proximity to the office.

"Okay, I'm coming right out." Jenna hangs up and touches my arm as she jogs past me. "Sorry I can't walk you out, Bart had to do the Heimlich on Dora Parks."

Instead of finding the exit, I follow Jenna to the small cafeteria area. A crowd hovers over Dora, who is sipping water.

Jenna arrives on the scene. "Are you okay? Thank God for Bart."

Dora nods. Her voice is weak. "Embarrassed. Cracker. Purse."

A siren overpowers her whisper, then the noise stops as doors slam.

Shirley hands Jenna a paper that I can clearly see says Incident Report. "She probably ate a stale cracker from the fifties."

Before anyone can admonish her, the front doors open and Wayne leads the way inside, holding the front of a stretcher. "Where's the emergency?"

My heart does a fast dance at the sight of Wayne in uniform. Jenna's about to answer when Jill enters, holding the back end of the stretcher. "Where's our patient?"

Watching the blonde bounce in, her flirty gaze resting on Wayne, I want to raise my hand.

*Engaged*

# Chapter Seven

Dora signs off on going to the medical center and I hang around the seniors, hoping to spend some time with Wayne. He shuts the lid on his box of supplies and heads for the door.

Jill zips up her paramedic jacket without looking at me. "Hey, Wayne. Are you hungry?"

He looks at his watch. "Not really. Jack Frosty's is open. Go ahead, I can finish packing up. I'll find you when I'm ready to head back."

My stomach feels as if I ate jumping beans. Maybe we can have a few minutes to chat.

Jill's dirty blonde ponytail bobs as she walks his way. "You sure?"

Wayne winks in my direction. "I'll keep busy."

She shrugs and exits, while Wayne doesn't move. My options are to talk to Shirley or him. Not a hard choice.

"Busy shift?"

He smiles and gestures for me to follow him outside. "Not bad. Glad this one wasn't any worse."

I match his pace and we walk side-by-side to his work SUV. "So, you're on break?"

Wayne opens the trunk and places the medical kit inside. When he turns around, he's inches away. The goosebumps I feel has nothing to do with the mid-October weather. "Yep. If I get a call we have to take it, but for now, I thought I'd talk to you. I've been hoping to meet up."

It's so hard to act collected when a handsome man is in your personal space. "Really? What for?"

He sits on the edge of the trunk and taps the carpeted area next to him. "I needed to follow up with you on something."

I sit next to him, crossing my legs as my feet touch the pavement. "Oh. Is something wrong?" Please don't say we can't see each other. Or that the seniors are right not to like me. Let it be good news.

He sighs. "I hope not. You might not remember, but at the race, when you met Brad and Jill, she mentioned you as a patient. Thing is, she broke confidentiality and protocol. I had to write her up."

"Am I in trouble?"

Wayne shakes his head. "No, not at all. I wanted to give you a heads-up. I haven't worked with Jill long, but she can be immature. I hope this doesn't happen, but she might blame you. She doesn't know that yet, my boss is going to talk to her tomorrow."

The butterflies in my stomach drop like lead. "Immature how?"

He cracks his knuckles. "Talking about you the way she did, for one. That's a basic rule in healthcare."

I bite my lip for a moment. "You look like you have more to say."

His laugh is soft. "Busted. I want you to know, not because I feel the same way, but because I want to be honest. I like you, Trish. But I think Jill has a crush on me, and I'm not sure how she will act when our boss talks to her."

Two days later, my head's reeling from all Wayne shared, what I've sketched for the storefronts, and what I need to accomplish at the store. The small bell at the register jars me back to attention.

Mom returns the bell to the counter. "Trish? Are you paying attention? Yesterday you had the closing report to the penny. Today, your numbers make it look like we were robbed overnight."

I feel like a toddler, remembering the time she caught me sneaking cookies to my room. "Sorry. I wasn't focused."

"I'm here today to catch your mistakes, but it won't be long before this is all on you. It's important."

I nod. "You're right. I promise I'll do a better job."

Before Mom can reply, Jenna enters with Roxy Tarantelli and Dora Parks, the two ladies from the senior center who could not be more opposite.

Jenna walks right to the counter, her smile wide. "Good morning, ladies. I found our last models and thought we'd take a chance in stopping by and picking out something for them to wear. While they browse, we could talk details. If you want."

Roxy and Dora make their way to the back racks with new women's merchandise.

I look to Mom, who nods, so I assume I can join the others. "We're starting to get winter pieces. Could I take some to the dressing room for you?"

Roxy is already holding up a winter coat with fringe. "This reminds me of our Rockette costumes." Her fingers trace the heavy material.

Dora leaves the new arrival area and heads toward clearance. "Any long skirts?"

Jenna raises her eyebrows as the senior finds a plaid gray skirt. "I'm sure we'll find something perfect for both of you."

The two ladies find a couple choices and visit the dressing rooms. Jenna joins me and sighs. "I worked on the program for the Christmas party. Were you going to create the coupons for me to place inside?"

I lean in so the ladies can't hear. "Do you feel okay? Do you need a chair?"

She waves me off. "No, Trish, I'm fine. Thanks, though."

"Okay, but you'll tell me if you need to sit or something, right?"

Jenna nods. "Promise."

"Alright. About the coupons, yes, I plan to do those." I bend down to the built-in shelf within the counter. "I already made them for the models. They're green paper stock in case they shop during a time I have someone else working. That way they will know the difference in discount. I'll do the ones for the program in red." I hold them up.

Jenna leans in. "They look great. Your printer is way better than mine. I think it's time to purchase a new one for the center."

I turn and see Roxy lift a sweater full of silver bling. When I unpacked it from shipment, I thought of her.

Jenna looks over to her and claps her hands. "I love it. That's completely your style. Looks like your size, too." She returns her attention to me. "I'm using the Christmas program and fashion show to introduce some of the improvements we've made with Howard's inheritance. We have new sound equipment, gaming systems for exercise, and by then we should have expanded space and updated office equipment."

"Well, until you get that printer, let me print your programs."

Dora steps out from the dressing room door, holding a bland brown sweater my mom must've ordered when she was distracted. "This is it. This is what I'll wear."

Jenna closes her eyes for a moment, then blinks several times. "Remember, Dora, it's a Christmas-themed program. I think the members want to see bright colors."

Dora pushes her glasses up her nose and travels back to winter selections. "How about this?" She finds a plain white cable sweater.

Roxy sighs and slaps her hand on her forehead.

I jump up and run to the next room where the sports equipment is. Once I find the ski poles, I present them to the group. "Throw a scarf around her with ski goggles and ta-da, she looks ready to go down Oak Mountain." I wink.

One by one the ladies smile. Jenna nods. "Brilliant. Thank you. And for the print offer."

I take Roxy and Dora's items from them so I can store them with the rest of the models' clothes. "My pleasure. Ladies, I look forward to seeing you both in the show."

Roxy flashes me a megawatt smile. "Trish, you were a delight to work with today. Thank you."

The trio zip up their coats and wave good-bye as another customer walks in. It takes a second before I realize the woman is marching right toward me, and I don't see a return in her hand.

The paramedic jacket and the swinging ponytail prove this is not a customer. It's Jill. "Hey, Tish. Just wanted to say thanks. I get to spend my weekend taking a refresher class because you got me in trouble."

Engaged

# Chapter Eight

Jill's green eyes almost have a Sci-Fi quality as she lasers in on me.

"It's Trish."

She folds her arms against her chest and taps her foot. "Like it matters. I made a mistake and I got written up. Know anything about that?"

"I understand that you aren't supposed to talk about a patient's history in a public place."

Her gaze narrows. "I know your type. You swing your hair and bat your eyes and think men like Wayne will come running. Thing is, I've heard your name around town, and your reputation is worse than the winters around here. I've been in town since you left. I also don't plan on leaving."

I start to open my mouth, but clamp it shut. Hot tears sting, but I will not allow them to fall in Jill's presence.

Jill doesn't let up on the eye contact. "Wayne's a decent guy. He's a father. The last thing he needs or deserves is trouble like you."

The door opens, and we both turn to look. Before I realize who it is, Jill shakes the wrinkles from her coat and puts it on. "Have a good day." With a flash of a smile, she's gone.

There's no chance to recover because Carla, Wayne's first love and mother of his child, seems headed right toward me. *Please don't let this be another ambush.*

Carla has her black work attire on complete with her logo, Untangled by Carla. "Hi, Trish." She stops at the glove table and picks up a pair, so I'm not sure if she's shopping or in-between hair clients.

"Hi, Carla." I walk over to the kid's section close by where stuffed animals need to be reorganized after a mom brought in her two preschoolers. I steal a glance and notice Carla visiting tables and racks without really picking much up. "Is there something specific you're looking for?"

Carla pauses in the junior department, which for our small region is only four racks and five feet away from me. "Not really. I mean, nothing I can buy." A nervous edge laces her words.

I wipe my hands, fuzzy from the stuffed toys, on my slacks and join her, which brings dread with every step. "Is there anything I can help you with?" Please say no.

Her purse strap falls from her shoulder to the crook of her arm. "Actually, there is. Do you have a minute?"

My words come out slow and shaky "I guess so."

"Noah told me about the race a week or so ago. He mentioned you went with him and Wayne."

This conversation is going exactly where I don't want it to go.

I nod.

She offers a thin smile. "He had a great time, by the way."

I arch an eyebrow. "Noah, or Wayne?"

"Oh, Noah. Definitely Noah. I mean, I'm sure Wayne did, but I wouldn't talk to him about, well, you know."

I don't think I do.

"Anyway, your name keeps coming up. Noah said his dad mentioned fishing and hiking, and maybe even rafting down the Sacandaga."

I twist a lock of hair around my finger. "For the two of them?"

Carla clears her throat. "My impression was you'd be part of the experience. And if that's accurate, I just wanted to make sure you're truly interested."

Her gaze appears strong. Way more intimidating than I remember when she pulled me over during her sheriff days.

"Well, Carla, I admit, these plans are a surprise to me. I'm not against them, I just haven't been invited. Yet." I smile.

She rolls her eyes. "He always was a procrastinator. Thing is, if he actually invites you, Wayne, that is, you don't strike me as an outdoorsy type." Her words are measured, guarded before she quickly adds, "No offense."

I'm blinking so much she must think I'm sending Morse code.

"So, if you don't want to do those things, and you aren't interested in the people that plan to invite you, well, don't hurt Noah. It's all I'm saying. I remember the day Ben learned you skipped town without telling him in person. I won't have my son experience that torment."

And there it is. New and improved Trish still getting the punishment.

I let go of my hair and place my hands on my hips, eyes narrowing. "I understand your concern. But I wouldn't ever hurt Noah or Wayne on purpose. I've changed. Grown. And right now we're all friends."

"Wayne seems to think you're as natural to the Adirondacks as a bear. I'm not so sure I agree." She folds her arms against her chest.

I steal a glance at the shelves. Log cabin knick-knacks. Black bear figurines. I've seen those my entire life. I didn't love them, but I'm an Adirondack girl. Now. "I'm definitely not a professional runner. And if I went fishing, I probably would catch a tire. But I deserve the opportunity."

"Speaking of, what if a big-shot job somewhere else comes along? Will you ditch them?"

And then my feet sprint right into my mouth. "You mean like you did by going away to beauty school, leaving Noah, instead of Wayne?" Because all of Speculator Falls remembers the trouble Noah got in at school when Carla put all her relationships in jeopardy with her choices. "No offense."

The door jingles but I'm not able to see who my customer is.

"I didn't abandon them. That's your track record here in Speculator Falls, Trish. I'm not saying it to be mean. I'm being protective."

I look to the floor because I don't have what it takes to focus on her. Not after dealing with Jill. The tears are falling, and I pray she doesn't see them. With a quick wipe of the cheek, I sigh. "Your message has been received. I hope you're happy with your shopping today." I step away and right into Wayne's chest.

Carla makes good use of the awkward moment and exits.

Wayne's hand cups my chin. "Trish? Everything okay?" His touch is warm, smooth, and as comfortable as a cup of hot cocoa. "You're crying."

I step back and shake my head. "Not the best day, but I'll be okay."

He arches his eyebrows. "Did Carla say anything to hurt you?"

"No. Really. She's looking out for Noah. I get it. Before she came in, Jill was here. She made it clear she has her sights set on you. And that she knows all about the real me."

Wayne sighs. "I'm sorry. When do you close? Can I take you out to dinner? I'd love to talk this out and make you feel better."

One glance at the clock, and my heart leaps. I get off work in less than an hour. "I can meet you at Jack Frosty's at six."

"Great. I have to pick up a few groceries at JB's, but I'll come back here and meet you. Does that work?"

I nod. "You don't have to do this, you know."

He winks. "You're right. I don't have to. I want to."

Be still my heart.

# Chapter Nine

It's not quite six-thirty when Wayne puts his hand on my lower back and escorts me to a booth at Jack Frosty's.

He leans in and his breath hits my ear close and whispers. "Pretty full tonight."

I nod and wave at Pastor Reynolds and Brooke.

Wendy places our menus on the table and grins. "Britanny will take your orders shortly. You two have an enjoyable evening."

My cheeks warm when Sara Bivins smiles our way and gives a thumb's up gesture. "I feel like everyone is looking at us."

He chuckles. "I'm sure everyone is thinking, 'Wow, what a stunner Trish Maxwell is.'"

I roll my eyes and play with my napkin.

"Why do you do that?"

I look up into those gorgeous eyes. "What?"

His husky voice has my full attention. "Roll your eyes. I haven't known you long, but you don't seem able to take a compliment."

With a sigh, I push away the napkin. "I have trouble believing them. For the longest time, I only heard them from my parents. I figured they had to say it. Then, Ben. But I didn't really pay attention to his kindness because I was too busy thinking about myself. For a very brief time, Kyle Swarthmore said things that any girl would want to hear. After I heard him say it to someone else, I finally figured it out that it was just a line he gave all the girls. You are the first person to consistently compliment me. Stunning isn't a word I'd use to describe myself."

He nods, and looks up as our teen waitress places two glasses of ice water in front of us on the table.

The girl cracks her gum. "Ready to order?"

"Hi, Brittany. I think so. Trish?"

We tell her what we want and once she leaves, I reach for my drink.

He offers a sweet smile. "Our waitress was my son's first girlfriend. Didn't last long."

"Teen romances rarely do, I suppose."

Wayne starts to say something, then stops. After a pause, he clears his throat. "Trish, I apologize on behalf of men like Kyle. Honestly, up until very recently, I wasn't much different than him. I've been upfront about my feelings for you, but I need to work on getting to know you. Showing you I can be trusted. And what I say to you, and about you, can be believed."

Before I can answer, his hand slides across the table, and gives it a squeeze. Of all the romantic gestures, this is the most comforting display of affection I've ever known. "I trust you, you've proven yourself."

He leans in, and I'm pretty sure all the ice melts in my water. "I wish you could see yourself like I do. You're intelligent, beautiful, kind, and creative. You help others. You aren't afraid to try new things. And you bounce back when it doesn't work out. Would you be willing to try something with me that might help improve your self-esteem?"

I rest my elbows on the table. "What do you have in mind?"

Wayne bites his lip. "Would you read the Bible with me?"

Okay, I didn't see that coming. "Sounds harmless. Why?"

"Because God's Word is full of promises about what He thinks of us. I'd love to go through a study or a list of verses so you could see how loved you are. Who cares if people around here don't love you, even though I believe they do. What you need is to believe God loves you."

⧗⧗⧗

An hour later, Wayne goes to the register to pay, and I want to pinch myself. Our dinner feels like a Hallmark movie and I don't want it to end.

Sara Bivins, Speculator Falls mayor, matriarch, and Ben's grandmother, reaches for my arm as I walk by her table. "Trish, how are you? It's so good to see you smiling."

Wayne's words are still fresh in my mind as I resist dashing away because I feel awkward around her for how I treated Ben and the senior center. "Thank you, Sara. Things are coming together slowly. I'm helping Mom at the store and working on an idea for a business that would help the Adirondack villages."

Her smile could defrost an ice sculpture in seconds. "That's wonderful, dear. If there's anything I can do to help, call me." She releases her hold and pats my arm.

"That means a lot. I will."

Sara looks to the front of the restaurant. "I won't keep you. It looks like Wayne is ready." She winks. "He's a good man. I'm very proud of how fast he's grown up in such a short time."

"He says any positive changes in his life is all God's doing."

Sara nods. "Praise the Lord. You two have a wonderful evening."

I wave goodbye and meet Wayne at the door. "Ready?"

He opens the door and a blast of cold air greets us. "To take you back to your car, yes. For this weather? Not so much."

Once he turns on the SUV and clicks on the heater, I see a few snowflakes dance onto the windshield. Although it isn't even November, snowflakes don't come as a surprise. They can happen any time after September.

Before he puts the vehicle in gear, he turns on the windshield wipers. "I did hear we could get a few inches tonight."

"Of course. I've been so busy at the store I didn't think to take my car in and put winter tires on."

Wayne keeps the SUV in park and looks at me. "Do you want me to take you home? I'm off tomorrow, I could drive you to work, even put tires on for you."

*Seriously, does he have a white horse nearby? Because he is a knight in shining armor.*

"You don't have to. If it gets too snowy I can go slow."

He shakes his head. "Trish, I don't have to, I want to."

It's my turn to reach for his hand and squeeze. "Thanks, Wayne. I'll take you up on that."

Our ride is relatively quiet as Wayne switches on the radio and Brad Paisley's latest song fills the car. The snow accelerates and I watch him navigate the windy road before the vehicle starts sputtering.

"Is everything okay?"

Wayne keeps maneuvering the steering wheel. The noises and jerking only increase before the car stops. "No. Can't be."

I arch my eyebrows. "What's going on?"

"This has never happened before. I'm out of gas."

I lean over to look at the controls, but I can't see where the gas gauge is, and I'm certain Wayne's kidding. "Funny. You just don't want me scared because something is really wrong with the vehicle, right?"

He turns to me and shrugs. "No, I really ran out of gas. I always check it before a medic run, but..."

"But this isn't your work vehicle."

Wayne nods and knocks his head against the headrest. "Right. I wasn't thinking straight. I was excited to be with you tonight and I didn't even notice the light. I'm so sorry."

"What do we do?"

He rakes his hand through his hair and sighs. "We aren't close to a gas station, or your house."

This isn't looking good.

"But, we are close to a house where I know I can borrow a gas can."

I cross my arms, feeling the chill of no heat. "Great. What house?"

"Will and Carla's."

The thud I hear is me hitting the headrest. "So you're saying the place to get help is Noah's mom? The one that had a little chat with me about not hurting her son?"

He reaches into his pockets and pulls out his gloves. "She'll be fine. Who knows, Carla might be asleep already. I really don't want to leave you here with no heat, but I feel like a jerk for making you walk."

I dig into my pocket and find my gloves and hat. "I'll go."

The snow feels like cold water missiles aiming for my eyes as we trudge through the fresh layer of the season's first snow. It's not too slippery but I don't resist when Wayne reaches for my hand.

"Please forgive me. This is not how I wanted tonight to end."

"Wayne, it's okay. An honest mistake. I'm more nervous about Carla seeing me and being upset."

"I'm telling you, the real concern will be Noah hearing about this and having a field day with this."

When we reach the Marshall's porch, a flickering light from a television is on, as well as a lamp near the window. Wayne takes the first step toward the front door and knocks three times. Within seconds, Noah appears.

"Dad? Trish? What are you doing here?" He opens the door and gestures for us to come in.

We take a couple steps inside. I don't want to get snow on the floor, and there's enough heat that I can feel my fingers.

"Um, is Will up? I wondered if he has any gas."

Noah's eyes widen. "You ran out of gas? On a date? Classic." He smirks.

Wayne hangs his head. "It's not like that. I offered to take Trish home because her car doesn't have snow tires, and I didn't realize I was out of gas."

Noah's still grinning. "Uh-huh. If that happened to me on a date, Mom would never believe it. Anyway, yeah, I think he's up. I'll be watching TV if you need anything after I find him."

A couple minutes later, Will enters the mud room wearing his orange hunting cap. "Hey, Wayne. Trish. Hear you're having some trouble." He reaches for his coat.

Wayne nods. "I ran out of gas. Wondered if I could borrow your gas can and siphon some."

"No need. I have some fresh gas in a can. Let's get it, and then I'll drive you there."

My boots weren't made for a lot of walking in the snow, so I speak first. "Will, thank you."

Before he can respond, another voice speaks up from behind. "Will? What's going on?"

We turn and see Carla in her flannel pajamas and robe, rubbing her eyes.

"Hey, sweetheart. Wayne and Trish need a ride to his SUV."

She perks up. "How come? Did you break down?"

Wayne looks like he wants to melt into the floor. "No. I, uh, ran out of gas."

Carla raises her eyebrows. "Seriously? On a date with Trish? Isn't that one of the oldest tricks?" She chuckles. "Didn't you use that one with me?"

If crickets could survive the cold, I think that's all we would have heard for the next minute. Thank goodness for Will. He breaks the awkward silence. "I won't be long. Don't wait up."

She manages a small smile. "Okay. Well, goodnight you guys."

⌛⌛⌛

Half an hour later, Wayne pulls into my parent's driveway with his car. The sidewalk is covered in snow and it's still coming down. He opens the door and slides out. Suddenly, my door is open.

He offers his gloved hand. "Here, let me help you."

We walk to the porch step and like magic, the light comes on. Even in my twenties, Dad still waits up.

I giggle. "So, this was interesting."

He shakes his head. "I'm embarrassed. This wasn't how I wanted the evening to go."

"It's okay. I know it was an accident, and it worked out. Will Marshall to the rescue."

Wayne sighs. "Right. Good ole Will."

I rest my hand on his upper arm. Even with the bulky coat, I can feel muscle. "Wayne. I had a great time tonight. It was a horrible day and you said you wanted to help me. You did. Thank you."

His eyes sparkle for just a moment. "I appreciate that. I'd like to do this again, soon, with some modifications."

I tilt my head so I can get a better look at his expression. At least he's smiling. "I'm curious. What changes?"

He bends down and grazes his lips on my cheek. "I'd like to subtract running out of gas."

I can't argue with that. "Anything you'd like to add?"

Wayne nods. "Next time, I'd like to give you a real goodnight kiss."

Engaged

## Chapter Ten

The blustery November winds plunge the temperature to twenty degrees and chase most people off the streets or keep them at home. The quiet gives me time to work on more store window sketches, and my sketch book is three-fourths full. The long stretches at the store without any human interaction leave me excited to take the next step with the drawings and businesses.

The bell on the front door jingles and a tall, late twenty-something looking male with blond hair enters wearing a paramedic jacket. Sadly, it isn't Wayne.

Brad makes a straight line to the register. "Trish, right?"

I push my book aside and smile. "Yes. Can I help you?"

He nods. "My boots are leaking. I need a good waterproof pair."

"No problem. We have some in stock. Follow me."

I mosey over to the shoe corner, Brad a couple paces behind. Once we reach the boot shelf, he stands next to me and smiles.

"So, you work here alone?"

I point to the waterproof style. "When it's slow. I'm fine."

He grins. "Yes, you are."

Ugh. How does Wayne work with this jerk? "I'll leave you to try these on. If you have any questions, I'll be up front."

He holds a hand up. "Wait. Are you seeing anyone?"

I take a few steps back. "Like I said, if you need any help with something from the store, let me know." I turn and make my way back to the register before he has a chance to reply.

Ten minutes later, he's placing a box on the counter. "I didn't mean to offend you. I saw you with Peterson and wondered if you were with him. Bro code and all. But if you're single, I'd love to take you out sometime. I'm harmless. Promise." He lifts his hands up in a sign of surrender.

I muster a polite smile. "I'll keep it in mind, thank you. One hundred thirty-seven dollars and fourteen cents."

He plunks down a credit card and I hand him the receipt.

"Thanks, Trish. Hope to see you again soon."

Not if I have anything to do with it. "Have a nice day."

He turns and grins. "Bye."

⧗⧗⧗

My growling stomach is the only activity in the store after Brad leaves, so I grab my purse, turn over my handmade sign that reads *Return in 15 minutes*, and lock up. The moon cookie isn't the healthiest thing to eat, but I make a beeline for JB's with my focus on getting one.

Ben's near the entrance and looks up when the doors open. His store has a couple customers, but it isn't that busy. Winter months are barren in a lot of ways, reminding me why I was so anxious to leave the mountains for New York City.

"Trish, hey. What's going on?" I join him in the produce section where he's unpacking tomatoes. "Cookie craving."

He chuckles. "Moon? You never could say no to those chocolate cookies with them."

I move closer to the crates and help stack. "That's one thing that hasn't changed. Another is how quiet things are around the Four Corners this time of year. The department store barely has a handful of customers each day. How about you?"

Ben sighs. "Thankfully, I have a little more traffic because we're the only food available for miles. People need groceries. I haven't given Noah as many hours, but so far, I keep busy. Are you installing games on your mom's computer to pass time?"

Now it's my turn to laugh. "She's flexible, but I think playing games would not go over well. Actually, I've been doing some sketching."

He stops with a tomato in his hand and faces me. "Like art? I don't remember you loving art in school."

I nod. "I didn't. I'm drawing out ideas to pitch to businesses around the Adirondacks. When I participated in that race with Wayne and Noah up north, I noticed how much opportunity there is if

72

storefronts were used for optimum promotion. The ideas are flowing, but that's all I've done with it. Draw out the ideas for different businesses."

Ben appears deep in thought as he handles a few tomatoes without saying anything. Then, he looks up and at me. "Did you draw JB's?"

My stomach lurches like I ate the tomato crate for lunch. "Yes." My answer comes out more like a question.

"Do you mind showing me?"

I bite my lip before nodding. "Okay. I need to grab that cookie and get back to work, but I'll run my sketch pad over and you can look at it when you have time. Be kind."

"You know me, Trish. I'll be kind. But I'll also be honest."

⧗⧗⧗

Knowing Ben has possession of my sketches and he'll be truthful, my nerves send me into deep cleaning at the store as I wait for closing. Shelves are dusted, I've rearranged the store front to advertise the fashion show, and I vacuum until it is time to pull down the shades and go home. Even the sugar from my cookie couldn't give me the fast pace to walk back to JB's and hear Ben's thoughts.

I saunter through the automatic doors. "Hey, Ben? You here? It's Trish."

Noah's at the register putting plastic bags on the carousel for easy check-out. "Hi. Ben's in his office."

I take a couple steps toward the back.

"He's looking at your drawings." Noah's statement causes me to freeze for a moment.

"Oh. Great. I'll see what he thinks. Thanks, Noah."

"Good luck."

Ben appears deep in thought, unaware I'm in the doorway until I knock. He glances up, smiles, and waves me in. "Great timing. I'm done. Have a seat, if you have time."

I take a deep breath and sit across from him. "So? What do you think?"

"I'm really impressed. It isn't just what you drew, it was your notes in the margins. Why these storefront ideas are important. How they will drive more traffic to the business. I loved that you used JB's for each season. You really showcased what we're about and have to offer."

My sigh is definitely from relief. "Thank you."

Before I can continue, there is a buzz and what sounds like a walkie-talkie. "Ben, Code. K. I repeat, Code K."

Now it's Ben's turn to expel air as he stands. "Follow me, I'm needed up front."

"What's 'Code K?'"

Ben turns around, his expression serious, one I remember from school when he was annoyed. "Code Kyle. I told Noah anytime Swarthmore comes into the store, I want to be up front just to make sure he doesn't try to manipulate Noah or who knows what else."

I tag behind Ben. "Wow. You two really don't get along. But I get it."

Ben ends in the dairy aisle as Kyle stands over the milk products. "Something I can help you with?"

Kyle turns, his long business coat slapping him in the back of his legs. "Ben. Trish. What a nice reunion between a girl and her exes."

I roll my eyes and stay silent.

Ben's voice sounds strained. "The spam is in aisle four."

Kyle laughs hard enough to throw his head back. "Oh, Ben, it's always comical to watch you get riled up. I'm looking for almond milk. It appears as if you don't carry the latest for those who want the best for their health."

Ben's tone remains the same. "I carry lactose-free milk, as well as items for those avoiding gluten. However, I'm out of almond milk. I believe my grandmother bought the last of it."

Sara Bivins, the most fit senior citizen I know who always makes a pit stop for donuts.

Kyle shakes his head. "You might want to rethink not doing business with me. Families are starting to order groceries online and have them delivered. It won't take much for your little store to shut down."

"If I lived in a major city. Those things aren't available here, and even if they were, it wouldn't be affordable. Now, if you'll excuse me, I have to finish talking with Trish."

Kyle extends his hands. "Be my guest."

Ben shuffles a few feet away from Kyle but doesn't turn his back, or his eye on him. "Trish, I'd like you to join me and Jenna for dinner this week. We'll work together and make an official proposal for you to start right here in Speculator Falls. We'll include grant plans that could get you funded across the Adirondacks. The next council meeting is in two weeks. You need to pitch this."

"Okay. But wouldn't it be a conflict of interest with you helping me, since you're on the council?"

A low chuckle from the cheese aisle distracts us as Kyle speaks. "Conflict of interest. That's rich." He walks toward us.

Ben backs up, the vein in his forehead bulging. In high school that was Defcon 5 anger for him. "Swarthmore, this is none of your business."

"Oh, c'mon, Ben. You know I'm teasing. Of course I'm not serious about you working with your ex-girlfriend on a village council agenda item when last year you wouldn't even work with your now wife on such a thing."

I gasp, although his crassness shouldn't shock me.

Ben's eyes are locked on me. "Trish, my offer stands. Between the three of us I think we can come up with something. I will give full disclosure that I helped, and if they don't want me to vote, I'll abstain. Promise."

Kyle folds his arms against his chest. "Hey, I'm offended. Trish, there was a time my business expertise was a magnetic attraction for you. I'm running businesses in Newark and central New York. I could help."

I roll my eyes and move to the front, toward the registers. "I can't afford you."

Out of the corner of my eye I notice Ben smirking.

Kyle stays by my side. "We had a good thing once."

"We were like the spam. A poor man's version of something real."

Now Ben's laughing.

Kyle gestures toward his chest. "You wound me, Trish. But, I think you'll reconsider when you realize how much we have in common, as much as you're trying to fit in here. You're a great businesswoman stuck in a dead-end job helping family. The bright lights of bigger things beckon to both of us. These mountains confine you. Let me help. Forget Hamilton County. You could be planning events for Westchester and Rockland counties."

It's easy to ignore Kyle's voice because it always sounds toxic. But he hit my trigger. Events. Planning. Counties with potential I never got to tap into. "Life in the big city isn't always the best."

The automatic doors grind open as Kyle nods. "True. But I know you, Trish. You have way more potential than you can live up to in these mountains. I'm just asking you to take these proposals and work with me for bigger opportunities. Don't partner with the small-minded newlyweds. You can do much better, and you know it."

I glance toward the doors and my eyes land on Wayne in his crisp, white paramedic uniform. He stands in the middle of the doors, looking at me. "Trish? What's Kyle talking about?"

# Chapter Eleven

On the night of my dinner with Ben and Jenna, Wayne texts me as I close up the store.

*So xcited 4u. Knock 'em dead. Thx 4 telling me u like living here.*

I punch in my reply. *Pls pray. I'm nervous!*

Thirty seconds later, my phone vibrates. *Call me later. Can't w8 2c how it goes.*

I stop at JB's to buy a coffee and moon cookie before driving to the Regan home. I need caffeine to get me through this dinner with Ben and Jenna. I think back to my text and realize as I start my car that I had my priorities right the first time. I need to pray.

"Heavenly Father, I need everything You have. I ask for peace. Wisdom. Discernment. I want this dinner to be enjoyable for everyone and for the business aspect to move forward. I need to know what Your plan for me is. I don't think it is the department store, but I'm afraid that might be your punishment for me because I was so against Speculator Falls for so long. Forgive me for all that. Thank You for bringing Wayne into my life. This night is for You to do what You will. Amen."

Ten minutes later, I knock on their massive log cabin door, and a snowflake lands on my nose.

I don't know how far along Jenna is, but she's beaming. No cosmetic company in the world could create a face cream to match the look she's wearing as she opens the door. "Trish, welcome. Ben and I are so happy to have you here for dinner."

I step inside and slip off my shoes.

"I appreciate you guys asking. I know it's crazy with Thanksgiving coming in a couple weeks, so it means a lot you guys wanted to meet to help me with that proposal for the council meeting."

She takes my coat. "It was a year ago I had to give my big senior center proposal to the council. I was so nervous. But, this is different." Jenna hangs the coat in the closet and gestures for me to follow her. "Ben told me your plan. The county needs someone like you."

Jenna escorts me to the dining room, where Ben stands. One year ago Jenna was his girlfriend. Less than two years ago, Ben's girlfriend was me. It's surreal to see him. Them. And me, in the middle.

I smile, thankful we can work together despite our history. "That's nice of you to say. But as you know, without funding, plans stay ideas."

Ben pushes my chair in, and then Jenna's as he answers. "Don't worry, Trish. After a good taco casserole the three of us will hammer something out. But you know, this sends a message."

He sits next to Jenna, and holds her hand.

I tilt my head toward them. "Like what?"

The two share a look and Jenna giggles. "I think I know where he's going with this. You want to stay in Speculator Falls."

I choose my words carefully. "Oh. That. It would seem that way, right? And I think it is."

Ben leans back in his chair. "You definitely aren't the Trish I remember. You couldn't wait to leave this place."

I look to the floor for a moment. "I didn't appreciate a lot of things." I glance back at the two newlyweds. "I ate a lot of humble pie in New York City. I thought that job and life were the answer to everything. Sometimes the quieter life speaks volumes, you know?"

Jenna nods while scooping this new-to-me recipe on my plate. "We're not so different after all. You'd rather be a big fish in a small pond, right?"

After Ben prays, I pick up my fork and take a bite. "Hmm. I never thought along those lines, but I guess so. I love planning things. Weaving businesses and ideas together to be more efficient and known to the public. That's my passion, and when I was in Indian Lake, I saw the need. We could use that here in Speculator Falls, too."

Ben clicks his tongue against the roof of his mouth. He always did that in high school when he was thinking. "I can't remember if we talked about this at JB's. Do you want to approach all councils in the county? Or, thinking bigger, would you want to visit all the tourist towns in the Adirondacks? That's a lot of driving, but that might be your funding source."

I take two bites of dinner before reaching for my ice water. There's kick to that casserole thanks to the spices.

Jenna puts her fork down. "You guys. Can we eat first and then talk business?" She looks to her husband, then me, rolling her eyes. "Oh, forget it. It would be hopeless to try." She grins.

"Sorry, Jenna. I'm not much help. I'm excited." And not just about the work venture. This casserole is delicious.

Ben smiles. "I understand. This is how I felt when I talked about the expansion." He nudges Jenna. "When I wasn't in a complete panic."

We chat about those chaotic times between Ben and Jenna as we finish our meal.

Jenna waves us off after dinner. "You two go on ahead. I'll clean up."

"Are you sure, sweetheart? I can help." Ben offers.

She picks up my empty plate. "Nonsense. The snow is picking up. Let's not keep Trish too long."

We retreat to Ben's den area to look over the drawings and ideas I put together. We're silent for about five minutes.

Ben's the first to speak. "Doing this for a couple villages probably won't secure any funding. Offering this through the Adirondack village, I think you have a shot. And grant work is probably the way to go."

I can't imagine driving all around the mountains in the winter to secure monies. Earning grants to secure payment to create the actual storefronts, seems an easier plan.

Ben taps the pencil on the desk. "There are a lot of logistics, but we can hammer them out before the meeting. You need more than storefronts. What else ties the area and the businesses together?"

I'm about to answer when Jenna appears in the doorway.

"Hey, babe. All done?"

Her smile seems pained. "I think something's wrong with the baby. I'm cramping."

Ben's face pales. "What do you mean?"

Jenna's voice rises. "I don't know how to explain it, but it's not a normal feeling. It's cramping. Something's wrong. I'm sure of it."

I stand. "Should I call someone?"

He races to his wife's side. "I don't know what to do. The urgent care center is closed. The closest place is Gloversville."

Jenna winces and leans forward, clutching her side. "Wayne. Could you call him? I think he's able to make calls and use urgent care after hours."

I nod, leave the room, and grab my phone, although without signal, it still gives me Wayne's contact information. I find their landline and thankfully he answers on the first ring.

"Hey, Ben, what's going on?" His husky voice almost makes me forget why I dialed.

"Um, Wayne? It's Trish. I'm at Ben's house, and Jenna has an emergency. We don't know what to do." My voice catches.

"I'll be right there."

Once I return the phone to the cradle, I face the two. "He's on his way. But, he'll have to know that you're pregnant."

Jenna nods, tears spilling down her cheek. "It's okay. I don't care how many people know as long as the baby is healthy."

Ben takes her hand. "Should I call Pastor Craig?"

My eyes dart back and forth as they talk. I can't imagine the fear Jenna must be feeling.

She nods. "I think it's a good idea."

Forty-five minutes later we're at the Urgent Care with Wayne, and Dr. Horton, while Ben and Jenna are in an examination room. Pastor Craig and Brooke meet us there, and the three of us sit in the closed waiting room.

"How far along is she, Trish?" Brooke's mint green colored eyes are filled with compassion.

"I don't know. I'm not sure they wanted to tell me, I just happened to be there when she and Carla were talking."

Pastor Reynolds voice is comforting. "Trish, I'm going to pray with Brooke. Would you like to join us?"

The two are holding hands, but they extend their open hands to me.

"Of course. Thank you."

Pastor clears his throat. "Father God, we ask that You give Dr. Horton wisdom as he checks on Jenna and this precious life within her. Give Ben and Jenna peace. Help all of us continue to put our trust in You. We give You our thanks, and give You the glory in Jesus' name. Amen."

"Amen." Brooke and I say together.

Fifteen minutes later, Ben holds the door open for Jenna.

Pastor Craig, Brooke, and I stand.

"Is everything okay?" I move a piece of stray hair behind my ear.

Jenna walks toward us. "We're fine. My dignity is gone, but the baby is fine."

Ben steps in behind her.

Brooke gives Jenna a hug. "I don't understand, but if you and the baby are fine, that's all that matters."

"It's silly, actually. I thought I was cramping. It was, well, we had taco casserole for dinner. And it didn't agree with me." She looks to the floor.

Ben squeezes her shoulder. "Basically, gas. But I'll take that diagnosis any day."

"Amen. We thank God just the same. We'll let you get home." Pastor smiles, and then turns to me. "Trish, do you need a ride home? Brooke and I can take you."

I open my mouth, but the door opens again. Wayne steps out and joins us.

"No worries, Pastor Craig. I'll take everyone back to Ben and Jenna's." He faces me. "Do you need anything from their house?

I think back to my fast dash to my car. I'd thrown all the papers in the backseat before Ben asked me to ride with them in Wayne's SUV. "Everything but the car. If you can just take me to my vehicle, we'll let Jenna rest and be done entertaining for the night." I turn to Ben. "I appreciate everything. I'll start researching grants. I promise by the council meeting, I'll be ready."

His arm is secure against Jenna's waist. "I know you will."

"Jenna, thank you for dinner. I'm so glad everything is okay."

She steps forward and offers a hug. "It means so much that you called Wayne. I really appreciate our friendship."

Once I step back I'm sure I have a goofy smile. Friendship. That has a nice sound to it.

⌛⌛⌛

Ben and Jenna exit Wayne's SUV as if it were on fire and head inside their home, leaving Wayne, me, and my car a few feet away.

I reach for my keys as I giggle. "They were in a hurry."

Wayne reached for my hand that has my keys. "Perhaps they wanted to give us some alone time."

My heart jumps. This isn't how I expected my evening to end. I didn't even have time to become nervous. "We're in their driveway. That would be awkward."

Wayne chuckles. "I have a feeling Ben's kissed Jenna a few times here."

I lean against the passenger door, giving us a little distance, yet making it so I can't leave just yet. "It's his property."

"Trish. I know this wasn't a date but here we are. Alone. The snow is falling and we have this spectacular view of the mountains and lakes around us. I'm telling you, this is a scene made for a romantic moment."

I can totally see how this smooth talker worked his charm with Carla Marshall back in high school. I certainly fell for enticing words that weren't half as sweet as Wayne's.

"You have a strong case in your favor, Wayne Peterson."

He nods and turns the car off. "Can I walk you to your car?"

"Please." Now my nerves hit and my response sounds like a squeak.

Wayne leaves the vehicle and walks to my door, opening it, and reaching for my hand. It only takes a few steps to land at my car, but I know I created the tiniest of steps to arrive there.

"So this is the part where I say I had a good time. But that makes no sense because Jenna had an emergency. I guess I thank you for being her rescuer tonight."

Wayne slides his hands around my waist and pulls me close in a dramatic move where I gasp. "Can I kiss you now? Or, would you rather talk out of nerves?" His tone is light and I smile as I place my arms around his neck.

I whisper, "I like the kiss idea."

He doesn't say anything, but he bends down and brushes his lips against mine. I tighten my grasp and draw closer, where our embrace doesn't stop. If a kiss could write a story, Wayne wrote a novel. Even with the cold, my toes curl inside my boots. The kiss deepens before we both step back.

"Wow. That---was worth the wait." He grins.

"Agreed. I better go before Ben and Jenna kick us off their land."

He reaches for my hand and gives it a quick kiss. "Trish, I feel like there's so much promise between us. You looking for a career based here. Me and Noah growing our relationship. The two of us exploring the feelings we have for each other. I don't want any of this to go away. Tell me you feel the same."

Kyle's mocking voice whirls through my mind about missing opportunities because of living here. I'm so shocked by it that I can't give a direct answer. "Kiss me goodbye, Wayne. Unless you want to keep talking."

# Chapter Twelve

The senior center lot gravel kicks up more than rocks. My palms leave a moist print on my steering wheel as I park and grab my fashion show folder. Standing strong against Manhattan executives never rattled me. Shirley McIlwain? She's a force.

With a deep breath, I push the main door and focus on the front desk. Shirley's on the phone, but we lock eyes and her expression changes from a smile to a look that mimics mine when I try brussel sprouts. She ends the call and keeps her gaze on me.

I give her my best smile. "Good morning, Shirley. I'm here to work on the fashion show rehearsal with Jenna."

She cranes her neck and seems to look beyond me. "Did you bring your materials for the storefront? Jenna thought if the rehearsal didn't go too long you could start creating whatever it is you plan to do."

I nod. "Yes, I'm all set. I left everything in the trunk, but I'm ready. Did you need me to sign in, or can I go to Jenna?"

An exaggerated sigh fills the air. "Of course you've forgotten what to do, it was such a short season you were the director here. Sign in, and I'll page her."

I stifle a giggle with a bite on my lip. Shirley could just call out to Jenna without paging her.

Jenna's black suede boots are percussion-like as she walks toward us on the tile floor. Everything from her smile to her red dress and leggings looks radiant. "Good morning, Trish. We're excited to see how the show comes together. Ready?"

I hug my folder to my chest as she leads the way to the stage. "Are the models nervous?"

She chuckles. "No. This group never says no to performing. They never let me down."

An hour later, Jenna and I re wrote some of the script and directed Dora Parks on her model walk. Bart Davis worked the kinks out with the sound system. After Jenna explained to Roxy that the program listed everyone in alphabetical order and not by professional experience, Jenna clapped her hands and gathered everyone around the stage. "Let's break for lunch. If Trish has time, I'd like to run through one more time, no stopping."

I step forward. "I'm good on time. We hired a recent college grad, she's more than capable to hold down the fort, especially mid-November."

Jenna nods. "Great. I'll see if the volunteers need any help distributing the meals. Trish, do you mind setting the coffee pots out?"

My mind races, trying to remember the routine. "Sure. Do you still have the volunteers fill them and place them on the cart?"

Dora's eyes widen. "Wow. Shirley said you don't even remember working here because you were gone so fast."

Another deep breath. "I'll go to the cart now."

Pushing the squeaky tray with wheels gives me the chance to connect with the seniors. Almost everyone has their cup ready for the hot brew.

"I can't believe it. Trish Maxwell here at the center pouring coffee." Mabel Coffey, retired realtor, winks as I fill her mug.

"It's been awhile. Thought I'd stay for lunch while we work on the fashion show."

Mabel takes a sip. "Good for you. It's nice to see you here. You seem happier this time around."

Bart cracks a smile. "Is it because of that paramedic? I went awhile back to a race in Indian Lake to cheer my grandson on and saw you two there."

These seniors don't miss a thing. "Wayne is very nice. I guess you could say I am at peace. I chased a silly dream for a long time, never appreciating what I had right here in Speculator Falls."

Shirley thrusts her customized mug with her name on it at me so fast it nearly hits my chin. "I'm confused. You couldn't wait to leave the center, but now you're content working at a department store?"

# Julie Arduini

The temptation to spill coffee on her plate is strong. "I thought New York City would fulfill me. It didn't. I'm realizing that there's a lot here that does. I guess that's the difference people might see in me."

My answer appears to satisfy them as Will comes around with the fruit cups. I push the cart back to the kitchen and wait for Jenna. But I get no peace when the seniors push on the doors as they retrieve utensils and finish the set up. I decide to stand off to the corner and stay out of their way.

The door swings wide, Shirley and Mabel plunging through almost side-by-side, laughing as they turn toward the pantry area.

Shirley's deeper voice is easy to recognize. "So, what do you think of Trish being here?"

There's a few clinks of glass before Mabel responds. "I think it's working out, she and Jenna are teaming together for the fashion show."

I don't want them to think I'm eavesdropping, so I take a step in their direction.

"I suppose. It's just, I don't trust her, you know? I have this fear she's going to have a better offer somehow and ditch the center again."

Apparently invisible to them, I retreat back to the corner.

Mabel coughs. "Sorry, I inhaled some pepper from the shaker. I disagree. What else does that girl have? She works at the department store. It's not like any big business is begging for her resume. I heard from her father that she hopes to make this storefront thing an Adirondack-wide venture." She clears her throat and steps toward the kitchen exit. "I don't want to burst her bubble, but I don't see it. Trish Maxwell remains a mountain girl with dreams too big for her britches if you ask me. But kudos to her for humbling herself to move back and even pour coffee here for an afternoon."

Their synced laughter as they leave pierces my heart and confidence. I want to interrupt their gossip session and let them

87

know I'm not the terrible person they make me out to be. But with each effort to put one foot in front of the other, the only success I'm having is wiping away my tears with the back of my hand.

⌛⌛⌛

Later that afternoon, the department store door opens with not just a gust of harsh wind, but Wayne. He strides over, taking off his earmuffs and leaning over to give me a quick kiss on the cheek. "I thought I could last a day without seeing you, but I was wrong." His grin is the perfect anecdote to all the things I heard Shirley and Mabel say.

"I'm glad you succumbed. Are you on break?"

He nods and places his gloves and muffs on the counter. "Yes, I have a few minutes. Thankfully, it's been quiet. How about you?"

I lift one of the glass maple syrup containers and smooth out the wrinkled price tag. "The store traffic has been silent this afternoon. I did visit the senior center earlier to help with the fashion show and it wasn't so quiet there."

Wayne reaches for the syrup and returns it to the display, cocking his head as he takes my hand. "Shirley again?"

"Things were actually going pretty well until lunch. I helped out and her and Mabel Coffey were chatting in the kitchen and didn't see me. They basically said my storefront plans will never work and they think I'll run again."

He takes his cold thumb and rubs the back of my wrist in a circle. "Oh, sweetheart. I'm sorry. Don't listen to them. You know seniors struggle with change. Your ideas are new. It doesn't mean they are bad, though."

It takes everything not to jog to the front door and switch the "Open" sign to "Closed" so I can wrap Wayne in an embrace and not let go. "Thank you for saying that. It really threw me, I don't know why I let them get to me. I was so rattled I couldn't work on the display window. I told Jenna if she doesn't mind me coming in after hours, I'd do it then."

Wayne bites his lip for a moment. "I'm off at six. Want a helper?"

Seriously, why am I keeping the store open when I could run off with Wayne? "It's not very glamourous. I have tulle and fake snow and just a lot of stuff to organize."

He lets go of my hand and backs up a step before reaching for his things. "If you're going to be there, it will be amazing. I'll bring a pizza."

"I look forward to it."

Wayne brushes a gentle kiss on my forehead and walks to the door. "To the pizza or me?"

A giggle escapes. "Yes."

⌛⌛⌛

With Jenna's borrowed key in hand, I unlock the center and start bringing in my supplies. The butterflies in my stomach seem to be on caffeine and I'm not sure if it's wanting to do a great job for Jenna, to show Shirley, or because I know Wayne's on his way to help. Fifteen minutes after I arrive, his SUV pulls in. The smell of pizza and his five o'clock shadow greet me.

Wayne walks through the open door and places the box on Shirley's makeshift desk. "What's the plan, boss?"

"How about we eat and I'll show you the sketch of what I'm envisioning. If it works, the senior mannequins will be decorating the tree I brought."

With a total of six slices polished off in thirty minutes, I push my chair out and make the trek to the front windows. Artificial tree limbs and mannequin parts line the area.

Wayne joins me and chuckles. "Looks like quite the fiction story."

I pick up an arm and wave it. "I know, right? Hopefully this work will have a happy ending."

With the sketch as our guide, we assemble in silence for a few minutes. Wayne stops after putting the top of the tree together and faces me. "What was New York City like?"

Talk about random. "Chaotic. Disappointing."

"No, Trish. Give me specifics. What did you do there? Did you have friends? What was your apartment and commute like?"

I drop the tulle and raise my eyebrows. "Where's this coming from? Why do you want to know?"

"I'm curious is all."

I blow out what's probably hot air as I try to organize my thoughts. "It was nothing like I imagined. My apartment was smaller than the closet over there. At least it felt like it was. I saw rats. A lot. Both the kind with fur and the kind that works the corporate ladder with no care for others."

Wayne opens a box marked decorations. "It doesn't sound fun."

I shrug. "I enjoyed some of the challenges creating events, but much of the time I was a 'gopher' girl. As in, 'go'fer this, go'fer that.'"

A "hmm" fills the air.

"Wayne, really. Why do you want to know? I didn't have a boyfriend there. Is that what you're wondering about?"

He hangs a small wooden nativity on a branch. "No, that isn't it. Honestly? I wondered if there was a ring of truth to what those ladies said."

His words feel like a punch to the gut and there's a shake to my voice. "I don't understand."

"I want to make sure you have no desire to return. I'm afraid one day you will get an offer to go back, and you'll take it."

# Chapter Thirteen

The oven door open, I'm greeted by the tantalizing aroma of mom's homemade pumpkin pie. "It's done." I reach for the potholders and take the Thanksgiving dessert to the cooling rack.

Mom turns from her turkey preparations. "Great. It's almost time to put in this twenty-pound bird."

I glance at the clock and see it's a good five hours before Wayne arrives for dinner. "We'll have enough food for everyone, that's for sure."

Mom chuckles. "If we have leftovers, I'll make soup for tomorrow. Maybe your Wayne would like some."

My Wayne. That sounds like something one of the senior citizens would say.

Funny thing is, when I open the door that afternoon, I'm tempted to shout a declaration to any passing traffic that he's mine. Poinsettia in hand, he's wearing a taupe sweater and khaki pants, looking like a Christmas ornament. His smile is wide and warm, as he leans over to give me a kiss on the cheek.

"Happy Thanksgiving, Trish. I really appreciate your invitation."

"I know Noah's with Carla and Will today. I didn't want you to be alone."

He steals another kiss, this time, a quick one on the lips. "Not gonna lie, I like this plan a lot better than being home by myself." He hoists up the Christmas plant. "This is for your mom."

I take the poinsettia and gesture toward the kitchen. "She's in here."

My parents are acquainted with Wayne because of community events, but this is his first time visiting as my special guest. Dad's carving the turkey when we saunter in. He turns and sees us, then puts the knife down. "Wayne, welcome. Glad you could join us."

Wayne initiates their handshake. "My pleasure, Sir. Everything smells great."

Dad nods. "I wish I could take credit. The carving is my only job. I think we're just about ready to eat. Your mom's in the dining room."

I lead the way, plant still in hand, and sense a hand on my back. I glance to my side and see Wayne's grin. My heart feels so full.

Mom's placing serving spoons in the dishes when we enter. Her eyes seem to sparkle as I hand her Wayne's gift.

"Hello, Mrs. Maxwell. I wasn't sure what to bring, so I thought you might like this."

She sets the poinsettia down in the middle of the table. "What a sweet gesture. I'm so happy you're here. I look forward to getting to know you better. I hope you're hungry."

Wayne pulls out a chair for me. "I hope you don't plan on leftovers."

Mom giggles, the kind of high-pitched outburst when she's trying to get dad to say yes to one of her high-end purchases. "It's all about the leftovers. Besides, with extra food, you can come again and bring Noah."

And there it is.

My hands shake as I put my napkin on my lap, because I'm envisioning using the cloth as a muzzle. "Mom. How about we finish this meal first?"

She exchanges glances with dad, who helps her with her chair. "Right. Of course. No rush. Unless Noah wants my pumpkin pie. Jay will finish that off by Saturday."

I narrow my gaze and focus on dad, who locks eyes with me and nods." Say, why don't I offer a prayer so we can start eating?"

The conversation flows as smoothly as the gravy over my mashed potatoes. Wayne chats in between bites without any hint of being nervous. I can't help but steal glances his way.

Dad reaches for the bowl full of stuffing. "So what do you two have planned after pie?"

I smile. "We didn't talk about it, but I'd like to take some pictures for my portfolio. I finished three store windows in town and they are lit up for the holidays. I'd like to have them included for my meeting with the Adirondack Chamber of Commerce."

Wayne takes a sip of coffee. "I think that's a great idea. Maybe walking around will help me digest all this great food. Plus, if I can help Trish's meeting at all, I'm happy to do it."

Mom dabs her mouth with the linen napkin. "I'm so excited. This is a great opportunity for you, honey."

After we finished eating pie and washed dishes, Wayne and I drove to the Four Corners and parked in JB's empty lot. He opened the door for me as I climbed out and adjusted the camera strap over my shoulder.

Once ready, Wayne reaches for my hand and we walk toward the department store. "I have an idea. Instead of only taking pictures of the storefronts you've finished, maybe also capture the ones that don't have anything. Match them to your sketches to show the potential versus the reality."

I lean toward his side and give a playful jab with my elbow. "You have great business sense for a paramedic."

He chuckles. "Just looking out for you. I want your meeting with the Adirondack Chamber to be a knock-out. Do you know where it's going to be yet?"

"They rotate so the same members aren't always traveling distances. I know it won't be Speculator Falls. They had their last one there."

Wayne stops in front of the store and releases my hand. "Hopefully it won't be too far. I want to know how it goes as soon as possible. I thought if it was close I could drive over."

Even as I work with the camera, I notice the sweet grin on his face. "You're too nice. Honestly, traveling allows me time to pray and collect my thoughts. If it doesn't go well, it gives me the opportunity to pull it together. I'm afraid if I knew you were around, I'd be even more nervous."

He steps back while I squat and click away at different angles.

When I finish, I join him and point toward JB's as our next destination. "I like how we can be honest with each other."

He nods as we cross the lot and pass his truck. "I'll pray while you're gone."

I stop and rise on my tip-toes to give him a kiss. "That means so much, Wayne. I know you will. That calms my fears a little."

"Then I will be constantly praying so you will have complete peace."

We take our time walking to the senior center, library, diner, donut shop and gas station. Flurries fall as we finish, enough that Wayne swipes his hand across the windshield to clear the snow. He opens my door, but doesn't move.

I raise my eyebrows, unsure of his motives. "What?"

"A few minutes ago you talked about how you enjoyed the honesty between us."

I nod. "Absolutely. This is the first relationship I've had where the transparency has been mutual."

Wayne takes my hands and squeezes them. "Same here. I need to tell you something."

My stomach tightens. "What's wrong?"

He clears his throat, and that only accelerates my anxiety.

"Wayne." I feel the moisture between our interlocked fingers. "You're scaring me."

He shakes his head. "Sorry. It's nothing bad. I don't think so anyway. I wanted to say that spending Thanksgiving with you and your parents was great. Being around you all day, I look forward to it, I hate it when it ends."

I want to wipe my hands on my jeans so bad. "Me too. It's been amazing."

"Phew. Trish, in the spirit of being open, you need to know, I'm falling in love with you. I think we have a future together. And I hope you feel the same."

*Engaged*

# Chapter Fourteen

Even though I'm tired from Black Friday shoppers at the store all day, Wayne and I agree to have dinner at Jack Frosty's. Once seated, he taps his fingers against the worn table. We look like a nervous duo as I knock my foot against the booth in rhythm to his movement. *Is he going to say something about how I bungled his love declaration? Wait for me? Say nothing?*

"Trish. I know we both worked all day, but your meeting with the Greater Adirondack Chamber of Commerce is in less than a week. You're the one who asked me to help you organize your thoughts."

I nod, paying more attention to his long weekend beard stubble than the notebook in front of me. "Sorry. I have so much on my mind. I'm having trouble concentrating." *Because I keep hearing you say you are falling in love with me.*

He leans in so he's closer to my side of the booth than his. "We're going to be honest, remember? Are you struggling with what I confessed last night?"

I reach for my water like a man just leaving the desert. "Okay, yes. But not in the way you think. I'm not freaking out at what you said. I'm upset at my response."

Wayne sits back and chuckles. "You mean that deer-in-the-headlights look and the, 'Hey, thanks'?"

I slide down in the booth with a groan. "It was as bad as I thought."

He takes a sip of water and then reaches for my hand. "It wasn't a proposal. I don't have any expectations that we will be calling Pastor Reynolds for a wedding anytime soon."

The air I let out in relief could fill a balloon. "I'm sorry. I felt like your declaration forced us to a new level I'm not ready for. I've rushed things before, and it didn't end well."

Wayne massages my wrist with his thumb, sending chills up my back. "I've been there, too. I was putting it out there that my feelings for you are strong enough that I'm not interested in anyone else. I hope our future is a permanent one. But pressuring you is the last thing I want."

I push my bangs away from my eyes. "Good to know. Let me confess I feel the same. No one has been the steady encourager in my life like you have been. With you around, I think I can scale mountains." I pick up the notebook. "But the reality is, I need to practice for that meeting. The sketches are ready, but I need to work on delivery."

He gives my hand a squeeze before letting go and looks at the blank page I have open. "Let's get to it, then."

Two cups of coffee each later, we have a good outline of what I need to say to the chamber representatives.

He smiles and points at the notes. "Time to practice."

I look around and notice the restaurant has emptied out. "I was ready to whine that I would distract others, but that's not going to work as an excuse."

His grin remains friendly, but he's not giving in. "I'm waiting."

"Okay. But I'll do it sitting down. I promise I'll practice in front of a mirror at home."

He pulls out his phone. "That's fine. I'll set the timer to see how long you speak."

"Good idea. Ready when you are."

Three minutes later I take a breath and wait for his feedback. He pushes his phone to the side. "Do you know how badly I want to kiss you right now? Trish, it was amazing. They will sign you up on the spot. I'm sure of it."

"Really? I said 'um' a couple times."

"Keep practicing. You know the material, you have to focus on the public speaking aspect. That comes with practice." He stands and picks up the bill Brittany left on the edge of the table. "I have an early morning shift tomorrow, so I need to get to bed at a decent hour."

Before I pack up my notebook and pencil, I glance at the cash register area and smile as I watch Wayne dig for his wallet in the back of his jeans. Everything about him and the Thanksgiving holiday has been perfect. I'm lost in thought when my text notification sounds. As Wayne returns to the booth, I flip my phone on and see the message is from a 212 area code.

Wayne clears his throat. "I'm all set if you are."

I bite my lip as I stare at the screen. "Yeah, just a second."

*Trish-Aiden Parker. Head's up, we signed a huge deal and will be hiring again. Interested?*

The gasp I give startles me as much as Wayne. "Everything okay?"

I throw the phone into my purse as if it were on fire. "Yes. Just a surprising text."

Wayne helps me put on my coat. "Not bad news, I hope."

Although Aiden was the one co-worker who didn't treat me with disdain, no one helped me pack my cubicle when I learned I was no longer employed. He texted me a couple times to check in, but by the time I moved back to Speculator Falls, I didn't mourn any lost friendships in the city.

I glance at my purse, and then to Wayne. "One of those generic texts that means nothing at all."

Once we leave Jack Frosty's, we amble toward Wayne's truck, parked on the street. Two figures stumble toward us, laughing loud enough that Wayne puts a protective arm around my waist.

"Peterson? That you?"

By now they stagger close enough I recognize them. I don't enjoy visiting with Brad and Jill when they are sober, much less inebriated, but Wayne pauses on the sidewalk in front of his vehicle. "Hey, guys. Are you feeling okay?"

Jill leans into Brad, but he's not a sturdy support. The two wobble to stay upright, and that only makes her giggle louder. "It's Wayne! And Tish."

I focus on the sidewalk. "It's Trish."

She glances at Brad and tries to whisper, but it's not a quiet remark. "Who cares?"

Wayne bites his lip for a moment, then exhales. "You two aren't driving, are you?"

Brad rolls his eyes. "Look who's the Boy Scout these days. You were more fun when you first moved here."

Jill nods.

Wayne clicks his car remote and the truck lights flash. "Can I drive you somewhere, or are you walking?"

The two look at each other and fall into a new set of giggles. Jill then moves away from Brad and steps right up to Wayne. My jaw tightens, and I move back a step, but Wayne's hand remains on me.

Jill's breath reeks of fruity alcohol. "You know, Wayne, wasn't long ago we left the bar like this. Remember?"

I hold my breath, bracing for impact.

Wayne focuses on Brad. "Do you need a ride? It's all I'm interested in."

Jill isn't deterred. "Well, I remember. Wanna know why?"

I can't help but glance in her direction. She's staring at me, her mean smile spotlighted by the street lamp next to us.

"Because Wayne gave me the best night of my life."

# Chapter Fifteen

The late autumn winds are no match for the chill from my heart. Wayne's jaw drops and he fumbles with his keys. "Jill, you're drunk and making up stories. Just get in the car. You too, Brad."

Brad stumbles toward me, close enough to nudge my side. "I think they have history." His index finger fails to point at anyone, but instead motions in a clumsy circle.

I roll my eyes and open the back passenger door. "Don't forget to put on your seatbelt."

Once Wayne and I buckle-up in the front, he turns to me. "There's nothing between me and Jill."

His voice is soft, but serious.

I force a whisper. "Yes, but was there?"

He sighs, and I don't like it. "One night I was in the condition they are. Somehow the group disappeared and we were left. I kissed her. It meant nothing."

A high-pitch giggle floats from the back. "Liar."

I focus on my breathing. It would be easy to believe Jill, but something in Wayne's tone tells me he's speaking the truth. "I wish we could drop them off at the end of my road and make them find their way back to town."

Wayne chuckles and turns on the ignition. "I know. We're doing the right thing."

More laughter erupts with noises that sound like kissing. Wayne and I turn around at the same time and see the two in a sloppy embrace. "Let's get these two somewhere safe, fast. I don't want to say goodnight to you with them right behind us." He winks.

⧗⧗⧗

Soft, soothing jazz drifts up from my car's satellite radio, but even Norah Jones can't calm my nerves. The fifty-mile drive to Tupper Lake seems like enough time to focus on my interview with the Greater Adirondack Chamber, and stop daydreaming about my last kiss with Wayne days ago.

Ninety minutes later, I park in front of the yellow building with four corner exposure. A wooden sign on the front directs me to the actual Chamber, as a pharmacy and sub shop also are part of the office block. The heavy door squeaks as I walk through, and a college-age girl looks up from her phone.

I clear my throat. "Hi, I'm Trish Maxwell. I have a meeting with Ed Sterling."

She looks down at the desk calendar and smiles. "Right. Let me buzz him. He's upstairs."

My portfolio vibrates against my shaky legs even when I try to stand still. *Please, God, let this meeting go well.*

A couple minutes later, a man definitely taller than six feet hustles downstairs. He thrusts out his hand. "Hi, I'm Ed Sterling. We're excited to meet with you, Trish."

My hand crushes under his strength. Before I can yelp in pain, his words register.

"Thank you, Mr. Sterling. Did you say, 'we?'"

He chuckles as he gestures for me to follow him upstairs, and he takes them two at a time. "Right. A couple of the board members were here to sign some papers, and I told them about you. They wanted to hear your pitch. I thought it was a good idea. I hope you don't mind."

I bite my lip for a moment, and hope my voice can carry confidence. "Absolutely."

The conference room isn't fancy, but it's intimidating with a long table in the center and a man and woman are already seated. Ed pulls out a chair on wheels for me. "Greg Joyce, Phyllis Keyes, this is Trish Maxwell. The young woman I mentioned."

I shake hands with the little strength I have left and sit in the moving chair. The three of them choose to sit across from me, and it feels like an office firing squad.

Ed starts. "Trish, tell us why you're here."

I place the portfolio on the table and open it up. "First, thank you for seeing me today. I realize you are all busy, and I appreciate your time. I believe my idea will benefit the businesses throughout the Greater Adirondack Region. I'd like to travel from town to town and create storefront displays to drive traffic. When I was in Indian Lake recently, I noticed few stores did this. I understand a lot of places cater to tourists in the summer, but, I think there is untapped customer potential."

Phyllis raises her eyebrows. "Do you have statistics to back this up?"

I nod and pass out the laminated papers Wayne helped me draft. "I created a market analysis using figures from the Pocono and Catskill regions. As you'll note at the bottom, they credit a quality, intentional marketing campaign with area storefronts as a variable in increased foot traffic and sales."

Greg glances in the direction of my portfolio. "Do you have experience?"

"I have a Bachelor's Degree in Hospitality, and a minor in marketing. I worked in events planning for a firm in New York City. This year I created storefront displays in Speculator Falls. JB's and the senior center both said they have had more visitors than last year at this time."

Phyllis keeps her gaze on the laminated paper. "Can that be attributed to your work?"

*Deep breath.* "I believe so." I push the portfolio to their side of the table. "Here are sketches, and the finished product, plus more outlines I did of businesses outside Speculator Falls, to give you an idea."

The trio quietly review the book. The silence is anything but calming, and I wipe my damp palms on my skirt. After a few minutes, Ed closes the book. "Very nice work, Miss Maxwell. What exactly do you want form us?"

"I believe approval from the Greater Adirondack Chamber would open doors for me. If you could include financing my work as part of their dues, I could travel and work on all businesses who request my work. I would let them know about me, and promote what I've done."

They look at each other before Greg responds. "What is your financing?"

"If you flip your paper over, you will see my proposed budget. I've allowed traveling, supply, and labor costs."

After turning the sheet over, Phyllis gasps. "Oh, my. That's quite high."

Ed and Greg are scribbling notes, and don't respond to her claim.

If I bite my lip one more time, I'm going to taste blood. "Remember, this is an Adirondack wide endeavor. Three counties. A million acres."

They look at each other again, and Greg gives Ed a slight nod. It's apparently the gesture Ed was looking for as he straightens in his chair. "Miss Maxwell, the idea is a great one. We need all creativity possible to make our local businesses the best they can be. Your proposal is well done, but I have concerns."

My stomach starts to churn. "I'm extremely flexible and would be happy to work on all issues."

Ed smiles. "That's great to hear. The first item is that when it comes to actual store front displays, you only have a few from Speculator Falls. To take on a job as big as what you're asking, we'd like to see a lot more Adirondack experience from you. Not just your hometown."

Phyllis pats the portfolio. "Your degree seems to be a better fit for a bigger city. I'm worried that if we were to agree on this, something else might come up more suited to event planning and you would leave us mid-project."

The churning feels like lead has dropped to the pit of my stomach. "I have taken that route before, and returned to the mountains thinking this is the place for me to stay."

Greg looks to his female colleague. "I agree with Phyllis. Even your budget is a big-city price tag. We can't afford that. I crunched the numbers while looking this over and we would be asking the chamber members for an eighty percent increase. They would never renew membership if we demanded such a fee."

Before I can answer, Ed stands, and I know it's the death knell of my hopes. "Miss Maxwell, it's a no, but please don't be discouraged. There are grants out there that could make for a great partnership between chamber members and what you have to offer. Keep working on storefronts in your county. Build that portfolio. If you stay in the area, I am confident we will see you again. I hope we do."

With one more painful handshake, I manage a weak thank you. The other two stand and walk toward us.

Phyllis offers a small smile. "Keep at it. With more experience, you'll do great things."

I reach for my car keys and squeeze them until my palm hurts. "I appreciate the time. I'll see myself downstairs." Before anyone can respond, I scoot out and race down, pushing quickly on the exit.

Once I'm in the car, hot tears roll.

I grip the steering wheel. "Lord, I thought they'd want this. I felt You lead me to this. I don't understand." Before I can find a tissue in my purse, the phone rings. I pick it up and check the number. Wayne.

His enthusiasm reaches my ears before I can speak. "So? How much did they love you?"

"Not so much." My voice has a nasal tone, usually a clue I've been crying, but he doesn't seem to catch that.

"What? No way. You have a great proposal. Your sketches are amazing."

I dab the corner of my eyes with a tissue. "They didn't think my degree matched what I want to do. They didn't think I had enough Adirondack experience. They hated the budget."

"Oh, sweetheart, I'm shocked. Did they give advice? What will you do now?"

The portfolio is the last thing I want to see, so I shove it off the seat and let it fall to the passenger floor. "They said I'm a better fit for a big city."

There's a sigh from the other end. "I'm sorry."

"Wayne?"

"You okay? How can I help?"

All the comments about my leaving, from Shirley to Greg and Phyllis, come to mind in a taunting loop. The hurt travels from the pit of my stomach to my head. "What if everyone is right? It's not the first time I've heard it. This was the only plan I have. I don't want to work at the department store forever. Wayne? What if they're right?"

# Chapter Sixteen

Nothing's going to make me feel better—not even Dad's invite to help him set up the manger scene in the Four Corners plaza. Since the interview a week ago, I've been moping around the house and department store, certain my dreams to work throughout the mountains is crushed.

Dad unloads a bale of hay from his truck. "How would you like to turn on the plaza lights this year?"

I grab some chicken wire, and work on forming a makeshift shelter for us to stuff the straw through. "I don't think so. Doesn't the council usually choose someone and make it a community event?"

He sturdies the wire frame and starts to anchor it. "We do. That's why I'm asking."

I raise my eyebrows. "The council didn't vote for me. There's no way."

Dad chuckles. "Believe it. They thought it was a great way to promote your participation with the senior center fashion show. To thank you for the work you've done on the storefronts."

I crack my knuckles. "To pity me because the Greater Adirondack Council rejected me."

He looks up from his work. "Trish. I know you're hurting, but there really is a lot of good surrounding you right now. The village is proud of how you've turned things around. Everyone's excited about the fashion show. Even if the interview didn't go like you wanted, you've still done a lot of things to make Speculator Falls a better place. The council thought you were the perfect choice."

I grab a fist-full of hay and shove it through the holes, before looking up at dad. "Really? I had no idea. That helps a lot. Thanks for sharing that with me."

He smiles and pats me on the head with a gloved hand. "No problem, Honey. The tree lighting and plaza festivities are Friday night."

"Okay. Count me in." There's a bounce to my step as I reach for more straw. "Do we need to decorate anything else?"

Dad gazes past me and nods. "Once we finish the manger scene, I need to pick up your mother and head to the office. Here comes Ben and Jenna. They signed up to decorate the tree the McComb family donated. I'm sure they'd appreciate your help."

I turn to find the lovebirds strolling toward us, hand in hand. Jenna has a bulky black coat, so I can't tell if she's showing. But her face definitely reveals a happy glow.

"Is three a crowd? I'm happy to help if I can as soon as I finish stuffing straw."

Dad wipes his hands on his jeans. "Hi, Ben, Jenna. I'll come back later and string the lights throughout the wire. I have Mary, Joseph and baby Jesus waiting by the tree. Trish, you can place them inside the shelter."

Ben smiles and extends his hand to dad. "I'll do the lights, Mr. Maxwell. Trish, we'd love for you to pitch in."

Dad waves goodbye and returns to the truck, and I fetch the four feet tall plastic Mary. After the figures are under the shelter, I join Jenna by the tree. She hands over one end of a string of lights so she can untangle the other end. "Ben tells me the council wants you to usher in the plaza Christmas displays this year."

I fight the feeling that it's a pity prize and focus on the council's encouragement. "Yeah, Dad just told me."

She stops maneuvering the long line of lights. "You don't sound excited."

A sarcastic laugh escapes. "I'm still pouting about my failed time with the Greater Adirondack Chamber. They were nice, but it was a rejection. Not sure what I do now."

Jenna narrows her eyes and smiles. "You don't quit, that's what."

Ben places a box of decorations next to me. "Quit? What's this about?"

Jenna doesn't lose her look. "Trish is upset because her interview didn't end up with a promise of money or employment."

Ben starts to chuckle, but it evolves into a full laugh.

I drop the lights and put my hands on my hips. "Are you mocking me?"

He shakes his head. "No, I'm teasing my wife. Jenna knows exactly how you feel."

She nods. "It's true. I presented the budget to the council and there wasn't enough information. I was asking for the moon my very first budget meeting. Ben asked great questions, and ultimately the money was tabled. I was so upset."

So she gets it. And isn't going to let me pout too long.

Ben reaches for a star on top of the box. "What did they say at your meeting? Was it truly a rejection, or did they suggest you try some things and come back?"

I take a deep breath. They aren't going to let this go. "They had concerns. I have the wrong degree for the job. I didn't have a lot of mountain experience. I only had displays in Speculator Falls. My budget was high. I need more in my portfolio to reflect the Adirondacks, not just my hometown. I was asking too much of the chamber members in their annual dues and should find a different method for funding."

He glances at Jenna, and the two focus on me. "Trish, you weren't rejected. Just re-directed."

"Did they mention New York City?"

I arch my eyebrows. "How did you know?"

Jenna walks over to me and delivers a playful punch to my arm. "It's your trigger. If they mentioned a fear you'd leave them for the city, you hear that all the time here. It upsets you. Ben's right. That committee sounds helpful. I think the last thing you should do is quit."

Her honesty stings as much as my arm, but I let the words sink in. I pick up the lights and work on untangling them without responding for a while. After a few minutes, I hand her the clean line of lights. "You're right. Thanks. I need to re-group. I owe you."

Jenna gestures me to follow her to the tree, where we start to hang our untangled project. "Joke's on you. I need to whine." She flashes a smile, so I'm not too worried about her issues.

I toss a strand toward her. "What? Jenna Regan needs to complain? I don't believe it."

Another laugh comes from Ben.

"Oh, yes. I know I'm being a big sister, but this is beyond frustrating. And I'm not just talking pregnancy hormones."

There's rustling behind us and I turn my head to peek. Wayne, in uniform, is walking toward us.

Ben jogs over and slaps him on the back. "Another guy. Tell me you can stay."

Wayne wraps his arms around my waist from behind and gives a squeeze. "I wish. I'm on break."

"Hey. Jenna's about to reveal a complaint." I step back, turn, and wink at Wayne. "I almost think it's her first ever."

"This I have to hear."

Jenna folds her arms against her chest. "I think my sister Meg is dating Kyle Swarthmore."

Wayne raises his eyebrows. "You mean Trish's ex?"

# Chapter Seventeen

As I dress for church, a flurry of texts arrive.

Wayne: *You're not mad that last night I referred to Kyle as your ex, are you?*

Before I can reply, Jenna messages me. *Would you be willing to talk to Meg? Let her know what a snake Swarthmore is? She won't listen to me.*

Ah, the protective, older sister. Always wanted a sibling.

*No, it's fine. It isn't a period of my life to dwell on, but I made a bunch of mistakes. He was the worst of them.*

Then, to Jenna: *What makes you think she'll listen to me?*

*Meg told me she admires you. I'm heading to church. Talk more later.*

I toss my phone on the bed as I look for my boots. Meg Anderson has lived in Speculator Falls for a few months. Of all the people to look up to, I'm definitely not the one she should put on a pedestal.

An hour later, Wayne waves from one of the pews toward the front, and I notice Noah's next to Wayne as I make my way to him. Haven't seen much of the teen since Wayne and I ran out of gas and needed Will to help.

Noah scoots over. "Hey, Trish."

I put my purse on the floor, not sure if this is awkward for Wayne, because I feel weird sitting by Noah and not him. "Good morning, boys. You both look handsome." My focus is on Wayne, who doesn't appear bothered that Noah's sitting between us.

"You look great, as always. Did Jenna find you? She wants to talk about her sister and that Kyle."

Noah smirks at the mention of Kyle's name.

I glance to the front. Pastor Reynolds isn't at the lectern yet, so there's time to reply. "No, but we texted earlier. I'll find her after service. Meg is an adult. I'm sure she can handle herself."

Wayne rolls his eyes.

I arch my eyebrows. "What? You don't think she can?"

An upbeat tune comes from the praise team on the platform, and Pastor Reynolds stands next to Brooke, clapping.

Wayne points to the front. "Sorry, we'll talk after service." Like that, the conversation is over.

And it feels like a bigger one is on the horizon.

After the worship time and announcements, Pastor Reynolds strolls to the stage, Bible in hand. "Good morning! As you look out the window and drive around town, we're diving head-first into December. Christmas music plays at the Speculator Falls Department Store. The village garage. Brooke and I had a group of carolers from the senior center visit last night. None of this is a shock to the kids I know. Christmas has been on their mind. They probably wrote their lists out weeks ago." He reaches for a bottled water under the podium, twists the cap, and takes a sip, as if stalling. Perhaps not wanting to say what God put on his heart. *But, why?* "Adults, I have a question about Christmas. Have you ever made a list and didn't get what you wanted?"

Noah chuckles. "Every year I asked mom for a BB gun."

Wayne leans toward him. "How does the saying go in that old Christmas movie? Something about you'll hurt your eye?"

Before Noah responds, Pastor continues. "Today, we're going to talk about Jeremiah 29, verse 11. Sometimes we don't get what's on our life list. I've had a lot of people visit my office over the years, and they have either two reactions when they don't get what they want. They get better, or bitter."

My mind instantly flashes to my interview with Mr. Sterling and gang. And the pouting that followed.

"I didn't grow up around here, so no one would know her, but I had a neighbor named Stacie. We were the same age, so we played a lot as kids, and went to the same high school. We stayed connected through our moms when we went to different colleges. Stacie was kind of a tomboy, and definitely like a sister to me. I was engaged to Brooke and home on a visit when my mom gave me an update on

Stacie." He pauses for another water break. "Stacie met someone at the church she was attending and everyone thought they were a great match because they were both Christians. Thing was, that was all they had, and it wasn't enough. But Stacie didn't know that. Because a few ladies told her he'd be a great catch, Stacie assumed the guy felt the same way--that they were destined to be together."

Soft laughter floats throughout the sanctuary.

"Turns out, the guy felt God calling him to be a pastor. He made plans to leave the local college and attend seminary. Before he left, Stacie and this young man hung out a lot. She said their goodbye was more of a 'See you soon,' so she took that as confirmation that this man was the one. Her husband-to-be, it would be a short matter of time."

I think about Ben. I never said goodbye, and learned later he assumed marriage was our future. I'd wounded him. Perhaps a fresh apology is needed.

"Months pass and Stacie kept busy. She was active in church, and went to the library. She told her mom she's reading up on how to become a pastor's wife. The church ladies encouraged her, mentored and prayed for her future, the one they were certain involved the young man. That was, until he came home for Thanksgiving break, looking sad. Stacie took her usual seat by him at church and asked, 'What's wrong?'" Pastor pauses, and the room is silent. "His reply? He missed his girlfriend, the girl he met the first week of school, the one he planned to propose to. See, no one let him in on the feeling the ladies had, and that Stacie felt, that they would end up together. He thought they were just friends. Stacie ended up devastated, without a plan."

Shirley McIlwain's voice echoes. "What happened to her?"

Pastor smiles. "I'm glad you asked. Like I said, she could have been bitter, or better. Stacie chose better. She believed if that guy was nice but not it, how amazing must the man be who God did choose for her? Stacie thanked God for that friendship and for what was to come, even if she didn't understand it all or know when it would come to pass. Three months later, she caught the bouquet at a wedding and agreed to dance with the best man. The rest is history." He opens up his Bible. "Whatever circumstances you're in that have you frustrated or disappointed because it didn't go like you wanted, know God has something better. His plan for you is perfect, because He is perfect. Let's open to Jeremiah 29:11."

The thin pages wrinkle as I find the verse and read it. *For I know the plans I have for you," says the* LORD. *"They are plans for good and not for disaster, to give you a future and a hope."*

*Lord, I want to be better. I don't want to be thought of as the city-girl anymore. I want to make a difference here. Help me.*

There's a soft tap on my arm. Wayne tilts his head as he gazes at me. "You okay?"

I nod, as the music starts up and Pastor steps forward. "Who is ready to surrender their plans for God's today?"

A new sensation flutters in my belly. Something almost magnetic draws me toward the front. When I stand and take slow steps to the altar area, the activity inside my stomach feels volcanic.

Brooke greets me with a wide smile. "Trish, can we move to a quiet corner so I may pray for you?"

"I'd like that." We saunter past the others to somewhere private. "I don't know what God's plan is, but I know what it isn't. I don't want to be known as the runaway city-girl anymore. I want to make a life here doing what I'm meant to do."

She reaches for my hand and squeezes it. "Heavenly Father, thank you for speaking to our hearts this morning. Trish is ready to put down all things from the past, including her plans for her life, and submit to Yours. Give her Your wisdom and discernment as she seeks You. Grant her favor that this plan would be revealed to her sooner than later. Help her realize all good things come from You, and the plan You have for her is good. Let her know deep down that

You are for her. You are good. You deserve all glory and honor, Father. In Your Precious Son's name. Amen."

Her face almost glows as she opens her eyes and lets go of my hand. "Trish, I can't wait to see what's next for you. I'll be praying."

"Thank you. I really appreciate it."

As Brooke turns to pray for someone else, I weave through the people up front to return to my seat. Mom dabs her eyes with a tissue and we lock eyes. She's like a gazelle trying to reach me, and is at my side in seconds.

"Trish. That was such an amazing prayer time. I want you to know first. I believe God's plan is for your father and me to speed up plans for him to retire. I'm going to be with him full-time. Get ready to run the department store on a permanent basis!"

Engaged

# Chapter Eighteen

After three outfit changes and two cups of coffee, I'm ready to drive to the senior center and emcee the fashion show. My stomach's been as jumpy as a kid on a trampoline since mom announced they were moving up their retirement date, but the show has my hands shaking, too.

Dad stops me before I back out of the driveway. Once I lower my window, he leans in. "We're sorry we can't be at your show today. You're going to be fantastic."

I manage a smile. "It's okay. You two have a lot to accomplish. We hired a great part-timer, so the store's in good hands. Hopefully, the show will be, too."

"Be careful. I heard the weather report on the radio forecasting our first December storm. It's supposed to start this afternoon."

I nod and wave as he walks to the house. *Okay, God. I really need Your peace today.*

Jenna's already on the stage working with the microphone when I arrive. Our clothing complements each other with her red dress and my forest green pants suit. Once she looks up, she gestures for me to join her. "Do you want coffee? There are bagels in the breakroom. Ben should be delivering light refreshments any minute for the show."

"I'm too nervous to eat right now. Maybe later. Are the models ready?"

She bites her lip. "I hope so. At the quick rehearsal Wednesday, they didn't know their cues or where to stand. It could be interesting."

I breathe deep and focus on relaxing my shoulders. "It's going to be okay. God's got this."

Jenna walks over and gives a quick hug. "Thanks, Trish. I get a little hyper during events. You're right. Not only does God have this, He has us."

"What do you need help with? Should I visit the women in the dressing room and see if they need help? Decorations?"

She looks to the door and clears her throat. "Actually, there is something. Ben's here with the food. Can you help unpack everything and set it up?"

I turn and notice that not only is Ben coming through the front door with boxes of cookie tins, Jenna's younger sister, Meg, is next to him. I face Jenna and cross my arms. "You want me to talk to Meg, don't you?"

Jenna's laugh comes out as a nervous twitter. "I owe you."

With a sigh, I join Ben and Meg at the table Jenna marked off for refreshments. "Hey, guys."

Meg looks up, her ponytail swings as she takes a cookie tin out of the box. "Hi, Trish. Congrats on being the emcee. It should be fun."

Ben nods. "Yeah. Break a leg, Trish." He chuckles for a moment. "Excuse me for a second. Jenna's waving at me."

Meg and I stack cookie tins on the table and discard boxes without saying anything. After the tins are all out, I open them and place the cookies on trays. "So, how do you like it in Speculator Falls?"

She pauses and faces me. "I love it. I miss Mom and Dad, but everyone is so nice."

"Are you working?"

She resumes putting cookies on plates. "I moved here after the school year started, so I'm subbing. My hope is to find a permanent teaching job in the area next year. Kyle said he'd keep an eye out for any postings, so I'm hopeful."

Ah, the open door Jenna hopes I'll run through. "Kyle, huh? What's that about, if you don't mind me asking."

She shakes her head. "It's fine. He's a good friend. I know a lot of people don't like him. I mean, Ben definitely has a lot to say about how I should never trust Kyle, but he's been so helpful. A lot of people that I try to befriend talk about Jenna all the time, and I want people to like me for me, you know?"

I definitely know what it feels like to compare myself to Jenna, and feel like I constantly fall short. "That's understandable. Did you know I dated him?"

She crumbles a cookie in her hand. "Jenna mentioned it."

"He was a rebound in one of my breakups with Ben when I was in college. I was looking for attention, and Kyle gave it. For a while, anyway."

Meg brushes crumbs off her hands. "I don't understand."

"He needed local connections to achieve some goals his dad gave him. He got close to me to befriend my dad. I felt used, and hurt. Worst of all, I thought he really cared and there was something between us, so I gave Kyle everything he was asking me for."

*Please don't make me explain.*

Her eyebrows raise. "Oh. Well, he hasn't been anything like that with me."

"Good. Meg, you're an adult. I don't know you well, but you seem to have a good head on your shoulders. Just be careful."

Her smile is genuine. "Thanks, Trish. I will. Even if Jenna probably put you up to this."

An hour later, decorations are up, refreshments are out, and the seniors are ready. I have notecards in my sweaty hands, trying not to smudge them.

Jenna runs her fingers through her auburn waves. "Okay, time to start. I'll welcome everyone and introduce you. Ready?"

"Let's do this."

She walks onto the stage to applause and whistles. "Welcome to the Speculator Falls Senior Center Fashion Show. We have several lovely models ready to walk the runway, clothes courtesy of the Speculator Falls Department store. The store's assistant manager is our emcee tonight. Ladies and gentlemen, please welcome Trish Maxwell!"

# Engaged

The clapping surprises me as I join Jenna on stage. I look into the crowd and see Wayne, whistling. Even Shirley attempts a mediocre welcome. In the back toward the exit, stands Brad and Jill in uniform. They aren't even smiling.

*I don't need their approval. The audience applause is enough.*

"Thank you, everyone. The department store is excited to partner with the senior center, and you will love our models and their beautiful clothes. Before we begin, make sure you check your program tonight. Each of you should have a coupon for the store, perfect for your Christmas shopping." I pause when I hear papers rustle and audience whispers. "Now, let's start with ski wear..."

Forty-five minutes later, Jenna squeezes me in a bear hug backstage. "Trish, you were fantastic. This was a huge success. Fred and Janice said this was the best event the center's ever had."

Even Dora Parks looks like a vision of winter in her fleece outfit. "The seniors were amazing. They did all the work."

Before Jenna responds, Wayne, holding a dozen roses, bursts through the curtain. "Trish, that was so good. Jenna, your seniors were naturals." He hands me the flowers and plants a kiss on my cheek.

"Thanks, Wayne. I have to find Ben, all this excitement has left me tired. I'm ready to go home. You two have a great night." Jenna winks and exits.

I clutch the flowers and inhale their intoxicating fragrance. "You're too sweet. Thank you for coming, and for these."

"Can I take you to dinner? Jack Frosty's?"

"That sounds perfect. I was so nervous before the show I couldn't eat. I'm famished."

He sneaks another quick kiss. "I'll go start the car and get your coat."

I nod and saunter toward the small crowd that's left. Shirley waves me over. "Trish. It was a fun time tonight. You and Jenna make a great team."

A lump forms in my throat. "Thank you. That means a lot."

She nods and pats my arm. "So, you sticking around town this time?"

The twinkle in her eye captures my heart. "It seems that way."

She offers a wide smile before heading toward the coat area. "Good."

Before I can bask in that kind exchange, Brad steps right in my path. "Nice show. Glad no one had a heart attack or anything." His smarmy grin gives me a chill.

"Merry Christmas, Brad. I have to go. Someone is waiting for me."

His smirk remains. "Wait. I want to give you an early present."

"I really need to leave." I start to turn when he grasps my wrist.

"Jill doesn't like you. At all. She's mad that she got written up, and blames you."

I shake my hand free. "Jill caused her own problem there. Wayne caught her breaking patient confidentiality."

"I'm not done. She had a thing for Wayne, maybe still does. In her mind, her trouble started when he started hanging around you. Be careful."

"Why are you so interested?"

He reaches into his pocket and pulls out his keys. "It's no secret I like you. I know, you and Wayne are a thing. But if that doesn't work, I'm here. And I want you to remember, I have your back."

Wayne saunters to my side with coat in hand. "Everything okay?"

Brad shrugs. "Just wishing Trish a Merry Christmas."

Engaged

# Chapter Nineteen

Wayne grips my hand tightly as we walk toward JB's Plaza for the tree lighting. "You're sure Brad didn't do anything out of line? He was on duty at the fashion show. I could have him written up."

*Jill and Brad facing discipline after chatting with me? No, thanks.*

I pause and surprise him with a quick kiss, but he returns the unexpected by pulling me close and extending the embrace until I gasp. "Who needs winter attire when you're around? I'm ready to throw my hat in the bonfire Ben started."

Wayne chuckles and gently wraps my hand around his and lays it against his forearm as we stroll to the outdoor Christmas displays. "You're changing the subject, but I appreciate the compliment."

The closer we are to the plaza, the more people surround us. "You're a great protector, Wayne. Brad's got an ego, but there's one thing he doesn't have that you do."

Wayne raises his eyebrows. "What's that?"

I try to couple my declaration with flirtation, with a bat of my eyelashes and a huskier voice. "My adoration."

Wayne seems impressed nonetheless, and gestures for me to follow him away from the displays and closer to the woods where we'd be alone. "What are you doing? Dad's going to look for me if I'm late for the tree lighting."

Wayne sobers, clasping both my hands as he looks to the sky. *Is he praying?*

I squeeze his hand. "I was just being silly a moment ago. You can ignore me."

He smiles, and even with darkness starting to envelop us, I can see his bright eyes exuding nothing but warmth. "Trish, I don't want to ignore you. It's been extra busy lately and I know with your tree lighting duties tonight my timing's lousy, but…"

My heart feels like it's in a tightening vise. My throat constricts. "What is it?"

"You said you adore me."

If my heartbeat were attached to a monitor, I'd probably short circuit the machine. "Was that wrong? I was kidding. I wanted you to know Brad is nothing. He wishes he could be like you. That's what I meant."

"I know, sweetheart. You're too good to me. I can't tell you how long I've prayed to have someone in my life besides Noah who would encourage me like you do."

I take a step closer, resting my hand on his chest. "I feel the same. Just the other day I was telling Jenna…"

Before I could finish, he leaned down and brushed his lips against mine for another lingering kiss. When he moved back, his voice was shaky. "Trish, I love you. I've wanted to say it for a while, but I didn't want to scare you. This is not a crush and it's not something I've ever felt before. I am completely in love with you."

My jaw drops, and my hands tremble. Before I respond, a loudspeaker from JB's booms throughout the plaza. It's so loud everyone pauses, including us.

"Trish Maxwell, come to the Christmas displays. Your dad is looking for you."

With a sigh, I reach for Wayne's hand and head for the plaza once again. "We'll continue this later." I lean in and quickly whisper, "But I feel the same."

Twenty minutes after we greet Dad at the displays, the crowd gathers to hear the high school choir sing Christmas carols and for Sara Bivins to deliver remarks as mayor.

Sara adjusts the microphone to suit her short stature. "Speculator Falls has ushered the Christmas season with a tree lighting ceremony since 1980 when my husband, John, strung the first lights on some trees he decorated outside the store. It's a wonderful tradition that we're happy to share throughout the generations. Tonight we have one of our own born-and bred-residents, Trish Maxwell, here to do the honors. Trish?"

I step forward and once again, hear clapping. *A girl could get used to this.* As I join her on stage, I notice Shirley whistling and clapping. Her gesture so sweet, it catches me off guard and I start to choke up. "Thank you, everyone. When Dad asked me to consider being the representative to turn on the displays, I confess, I didn't feel worthy. As a little girl, it seemed like the people chosen for that honor had made great strides to make Speculator Falls a success."

Noah cups his hands around his mouth. "You're a success, Trish!"

My cheeks warm with all the attention. "Thank you. It is an honor to participate tonight, because Christmas is a time of celebration and rejoicing. I can't think of any place I'd rather be, or any group of people, than with my friends here. So, let's start the season with light!"

Applause follows me as I jog over to the electronic board Ben and dad created. "Will you count down with me? 3. 2. 1!" I hit the switches the men highlighted in yellow for me. A circle of trees and other Christmas-themed light displays come alive just as snow starts to fall. The sight is so *It's a Wonderful Life* that tears slide down my cheeks. "Now, Ben and Jenna Regan have a few words to share."

Ben keeps his hand on Jenna's back as they stand next to me. She clears her throat and starts to speak. "One of the traditions we have beyond the tree lighting is for JB's to offer free hot chocolate, cider, roasted chestnuts and donuts around the bonfire. We hope you'll join us. Before we enjoy the refreshments, Ben and I wanted to share our good news." She pauses and looks at Ben, who's grinning. "We wanted to announce that we're going to have a baby!"

Gasps, oohs, and ahhs fill the air.

Bart Davis is the first to speak. "When are you due?"

Jenna can barely stand still she seems so excited. "The twelfth of June. I wanted to clear the first trimester before telling everyone. My doctor said everything's great, and we thought tonight's a great night to share. Now, let's enjoy the bonfire and light displays!"

The crowd disperses and Wayne nudges me. "Great job with the tree lighting, Trish. You represented Speculator Falls well. Did you want to go to the bonfire?"

"Sure. I've been craving one of JB's chocolate donuts. I think dad has some chairs set up."

Wayne rubs his stomach. "That sounds good. Ready?"

We march behind JB's where there's a clearing and men tending the roaring fire. Mom's near the donut table, so I point and we move toward the line. Before reaching it, there's a tap on my shoulder.

"Excuse me? Miss Maxwell?"

I turn and face Ed Sterling, the man from my failed interview with the Greater Adirondack Chamber. "Yes, hello. What brings you to Speculator Falls?"

He cocks his head toward the fire. "Visiting my sister and nephew. They live in Piseco and invited me here for the festivities. I had no idea you were so beloved by the community here. That was certainly understated in your resume."

I glance at Wayne, who shrugs.

Ed continues before I can introduce him to my boyfriend. "Have you been working on more storefronts? If you build your portfolio and consider locating the funding yourself through grants and individual businesses, I'm confident we can put the chamber behind your work."

I bite my lip before responding. "You're saying being the Speculator Falls tree lighting representative enhances my chances to be supported by the chamber?"

Mr. Sterling nods. "Your communications with us led the chamber to believe you were starting out with no real ties to the Adirondacks. Seeing you here and so well received does change my perspective for the better. You do need to expand your portfolio beyond Speculator Falls, but I don't see that as a problem." He looks over to the crowd near the fire. "I need to go, but Miss Maxwell, stay in touch. It appears that you have a bright future in the

Julie Arduini

Adirondacks."

*Engaged*

# Chapter Twenty

The Valentine card selection at JB's doesn't convey my feelings for Wayne. Although we see each other every day for dinners or movies at my house, we're not a couple who are too serious or sappy, especially now that the "I love you" declaration is out of the way. The other cards are sarcastic. I only have a couple hours before our romantic dinner at Harmony Lodge.

"Trish Maxwell, what are you doing shopping for a card last minute?"

I turn and find Shirley and her thick glasses staring down at me. "I've been looking for weeks, I can't find what I want to say."

A slow smile appears. "Do you think Ben's going to order something better as the date gets closer? I have an idea, if you're interested."

"Go on. Are you going to take me to a back alley and show me some rejected Hallmark cards?"

A hearty laugh echoes throughout the store. "You're funnier than I remember. I'll be home the rest of the day. Stop by. I create cards, even thought about asking Jenna if we could offer it as an activity at the center. There's room for you to write on them."

I tap my chin as I think about my schedule. "That's a great idea, thank you. You're pretty awesome, Shirley."

"I was pretty hard on you. You've done a fantastic job making our village look better. Forgive me for not giving you a chance."

There's a miracle in the middle of JB's when we hug. "There's nothing to forgive. I'll see you soon."

Three hours later, Wayne and I have a mountain-view table and a basket of fresh bread between us. Shirley's hand-crafted card awaits in my purse for the perfect moment.

Wayne hands me a menu. "I feel like we haven't had time to talk since Christmas. It's been busy, hasn't it?"

I open it up and look at the appetizer options before concentrating on Wayne's wavy midnight-colored hair. "The store's usually quiet after the New Year but customers are using their coupons from the fashion show. I even had to call our college part-timer in a couple afternoons. And you, I think it's great that you're getting more shifts. Even your boss said he's so impressed with you he wants to give you as many opportunities as possible."

"You're too kind. It's also probably because Brad was written up for not stocking and cleaning the ambulance."

We order and he turns around and fishes around his coat pocket. He produces a card that's crumpled. "Sorry. I almost forgot it, and I stuffed it in my coat on my way to pick you up. All the words are true, though."

I slide it out of the envelope and recognize it as one of my card choices from JB's. Somehow, from him, it doesn't seem so generic.

*Trish,*

*Doing life with you is more than I deserve. I love you and hope you'll save room for chocolate. Wayne*

"I love you, too. There aren't enough words to explain how happy I've been, and you have everything to do with it. Now, give me a second." I hold up a finger and deliver my card. Shirley even insisted I put confetti she made inside, so it spills out as Wayne opens it.

"There's no way this was at JB's. Trish, it's just like you."

I lean in. "How's that?" He rises and moves in for a quick kiss. "Beautiful."

As he sits back down, he shifts around and seems to look past me. "I think Jenna's sister is here with Swarthmore."

It's hard not to swivel around as fast as an oiled chair in a diner. Sure enough, Meg and Kyle are across the restaurant. They're holding hands and gazing at each other.

Wayne shakes his head. "That's nauseating."

"They look genuinely happy, though."

He chuckles. "Maybe because Kyle hasn't made Meg pay for the meal yet."

"Funny. Let's hope Ben and Jenna don't come here tonight. She's still not on board with her little sister dating Kyle." The waitress interrupts, placing our plates in front of us. "Now, let's forget about them and enjoy our night."

After our dinner, Wayne opens the truck door as I climb in. "Would you like to come over to my place? I forgot the chocolates there."

*He seems extra nervous for a simple Valentine's date.* "Can we grab the chocolates and go to my house? Since Pastor's sermon on having a pure heart and life, I don't want any temptation. At least going to my place means parents will be around. And you in that red sweater and that hair, it's probably a wise plan."

He nods, closes the passenger door and makes his way inside, starting the ignition. "Okay. I did want to talk though. It's kind of serious."

*Did I gasp? I hope my panic isn't showing. Is this night leading to a proposal?* "My parents aren't going to be sitting with us or anything. Is that a problem?"

The engine roars to life and I can't see or hear his answer. My dinner rides like a tsunami through my stomach.

Twenty minutes and a wave hello to my parents in the office, Wayne hands me a box of chocolates and a dozen roses. "I meant to have everything ready for you before dinner, but I had a lot on my mind."

I gesture for him to join me on the couch. "You didn't need to do any of this. Thank you, I love it." Before he can reply, I give him a peck on a cheek. "Now, why are you are so anxious?"

He runs a hand through those luscious curls. "Okay. Here goes. We've been dating for a few months. The 'I love you' has been said and returned. We attend church together."

This sure feels like destination proposal. My throat feels like cotton and woodchips. "We're in a great place. I never thought I'd meet someone as amazing as you."

He smiles and reaches for my hand. He's shaking. "I'm so happy to hear you say that. I confess, I'm thinking about a future with you."

Oh, my. This is real.

"There's one thing left."

Can he hear my heartbeat? Can Albany? The space station? "I'm listening."

"If we were to marry, we'd be a ready-made family. Although Noah's not with me all the time, he is my son. We haven't done a lot of things together and he really doesn't know you. My question is, are you willing to get to know him better?"

My ears ring out of fear and misunderstanding. "Come again?"

"Trish, we have something really good here. I'm praying for us."

My voice cracks. "But?"

"But, Noah has to be part of us. He's a part of me. Are you interested in developing a relationship with him? Not just as a friend, but with the understanding if we marry, you also gain a son?"

# Chapter Twenty-One

Noah's whistle echoes throughout the Tupper Lake bank lobby as we work on a spring display. He holds up pastel tulle. "What's this colored stuff? Fish net?"

I stifle a giggle. "Not exactly, but keep draping it over those columns. It looks great."

He nods and puts his earbuds back in. Not quite the perfect scenario to get to know him better, but he's helping me and not complaining. Win.

After a couple hours of steady work, I tap him on the shoulder. "Do you want to get lunch?"

Noah removes the earpieces. "Did you say lunch?"

"I did. We're almost done here, and then after a break, we can assemble the design for the daycare down the street. Does that sound good?"

"Yep. Is it okay if we find a hamburger place? I'm kind of sick of pizza."

Half an hour later we're in a booth at the only diner I saw on the main street. It's hard not to look at their front window and picture a display, but my focus has to be Noah.

I rest my arms on the Formica table. "Thanks for doing this today. I know you probably had more exciting plans in mind on your winter break."

He takes a sip of his pop and shrugs. "Not really. I think Dad's tired of me playing video games. That was the only thing I was going to do."

"What ones do you play?"

His face brightens. "Almost anything. Combat, racing, football. Do you do any of that stuff?"

I open my mouth, but nothing comes out. A ball of panic starts in my mind and travels throughout my body. "I don't. I'm the only child in the family and my parents wanted me to read. Do you like books?"

Noah shrugs. "Not really." His face brightens. "Music. Everyone loves that. What do you listen to?"

Okay, we can find common ground here. "Soft pop. I guess because it plays throughout the department store. Celine Dion, Madonna's older stuff. Contemporary Christian music. Worship songs. You know, Hillsong."

His smile turns to a flat line, like our bonding. "Country."

We both sigh.

He finishes up his burger and I pick at my salad. *You're not step-mom material. You can't even talk to a teen.* Pushing my plate aside, I forge into new territory. "Tell me something about you and your dad that would surprise me."

Noah grins. "If we can't find anything on TV during a snowstorm, we watch The Hallmark channel."

I stifle a laugh. "Good one. What do you love most about him?"

"He moved here to get to know me."

The fear disappears as we keep chatting. Noah stretches and asks, "Do you ever plan to run a race with us again?"

"Why? Are you implying I'm not good?"

He nods. "You were a mess that day. Here's a tough one."

I reach for the bill and stand. "Go for it."

"What job do you plan to keep? The department store, or what we're doing today?"

Okay, Noah's a straight shooter like his mom. "I want the opportunity to create window displays across the Adirondacks. I hope that works out. But, my parents are getting ready for my dad to retire, so they need me at the store. It's complicated."

He rises and puts on his coat. "Sounds like it. Last question."

"I'm ready."

Noah's stare is laser focused. "Did Dad put you up to this as a test to see if we get along well enough for you to become my step-mom?"

☷☷☷

Three days later, I'm back in Tupper Lake at the library. I now have businesses in Speculator Falls, Piseco, and Tupper Lake for my portfolio. Another village and I should be able to call Ed Sterling and show him my updated work.

Noah's in the corner, untangling lights, muttering under his breath. "Trish, how bad do you need these?" He holds up the tangled mass of electricity.

"It's important. Let me staple this letter to the display board and I'll help."

Before he can respond, my phone rings. I look at the screen, noticing it's a New York City area code, and Aiden Parker's name. "Excuse me a second, Noah. I need to take this."

I jog to an empty conference room and swipe to answer. "Hey, Aiden. Need to vent about a project?"

His words come so fast I can barely process. "Big shake-up. CEO is gone. Board president, resigned. New leadership promoted me and asked me to name my partner."

I saunter to the door and peek out to see Noah still holding on to the lights. "That's great, Aiden. Who are you going with? Prescott? Annette Rhoades?"

There's such a long pause that I check to make sure the call is still active. "Aiden?"

"You, Trish. I want to hire you."

I'm speechless. *Did he just offer me a job in the City?*

"I know your job last time wasn't what you thought. A lot of that was mis-management. You have the ambition, and your ideas when we led the Stevenson project were good. Really good."

I pace an imprint into the carpet. "Aiden, I'm flattered."

"Don't say no. We would get an office and share an assistant. I can help you find an apartment. At least meet with me, won't you? I'll even meet half-way. Lunch in Binghamton?"

My knees weaken. "I, I don't know. This is a shock."

"Meet me in Binghamton. Let me show you the projects I'm leading. If you say yes, we're co-leads. The company is heading in the right direction. I feel really good about this."

What's the harm in lunch? "Okay. Monday. I'm craving a chicken spiedie, so let's meet at the Rib Pit. One?" I can taste the marinated chicken on a sub roll already.

"You got it. Thanks, Trish. It's a great opportunity. You don't want to pass it up."

When I return to the lobby, Noah's made headway and didn't even seem to notice I was gone longer than a minute. "Great job. You didn't even need my help."

He rolls his eyes. "No more untangling today. What else are we doing?"

"Place the presentation board in the center, hang the lights, and done."

"Cool. Then we go home?"

Dread feels like it's filling the creases in my forehead. "Yep. I also have to call your dad."

As soon as we're in my car, I hit Wayne's number and he answers on the second ring.

"Hey, Honey. I wondered if you two were about done."

My voice cracks. "We are. Headed back. Do you have a few minutes for us to talk tonight? Privately?"

His words come out slow and measured. "Sure. Everything okay?"

I glance at Noah, who smiles.

"I'm not sure."

# Chapter Twenty-Two

My knees shake as I wrap my arms around Wayne's chest as he navigates his four-wheeler across Lake Pleasant. Ice fishing isn't the most romantic plan, but with the news I need to deliver, it gives us needed privacy.

Wayne shuts the engine off and reaches for the cooler he loaded in the back. "You okay, Trish? I thought for a second you were going to bruise my ribs."

My nervous laughter sounds more like a shiver. "I'm a little anxious about the ice breaking."

He winks as he sets up the camping chairs. "It's ten-below zero, the ice is six inches thick. We'll be okay."

I stand with my gloved hands stuffed in my coat pockets. "Good. Ice fishing isn't something I embraced growing up."

Wayne's definitely the expert as he drills a hole and produces a slotted ladle to scoop out excess ice chunks. "My dad would take me to Saranac Lake when I was a kid. Ice fishing's peaceful, although I wouldn't count on fish for our dinner." He chuckles as he hands me a fishing pole.

*I'm not sure he's going to want me to stick around for dinner.* "Then what would I do?"

He picks up his drill. "Take a seat and stick the pole in the water. I'm making my hole." Wayne looks over as I oblige. "I've been meaning to ask, have you called that Ed guy about your portfolio? You and Noah covered some great Adirondack territory creating those displays."

I nearly lose my grip on the pole and almost drop it into the hole. "I finished updating it last night. I haven't called yet."

Wayne nods as he finishes up and takes a seat. "I don't know how he could say no to you this time. You did everything he suggested."

I bite my lip, but can barely feel it. "Right. Along that line, I have something work related to talk to you about."

He leans back with pole in hand. "Sure. What's going on?"

I sigh. *Lord, let this conversation go well.* "Aiden Parker called me the other day."

Wayne leans forward. "Isn't that the guy you worked with in New York?"

I nod. "Seems they're in transition where I used to work. The old management is gone and he's been promoted to Project Manager. He's really excited."

"Great. Is that why he called, to tell you about his job?"

"Kind of. He wants me to be on his team. I guess there are new projects coming up that he feels I would be a perfect fit to work with him as his creative lead."

Wayne is on the edge of the chair, almost ready to tip it over. "That was nice of him to think of you. What did he say when you turned him down?"

The air is still. Not even birds are responding to that question.

I glance at him, his jawline, and his curls spilling out under the orange knitted hat. "He asked if I'd meet him for lunch to learn more."

Wayne's eyebrows form a V.

"It's just a lunch in Binghamton. I didn't see any harm in finding out what he has to say."

"Trish, why would you go and waste his time? You're giving him false hope. He's going to think he's luring you into the job."

More silence as he works his jaw muscled through clenched teeth.

"It sounds like there has been a lot of change and Aiden's excited."

"From what I'm hearing, your friend isn't the only one excited. Are you considering this? Why would you go all that way if you weren't tempted to take the job?"

My sigh turns into a frosty cloud that dissipates. "What Aiden described sounds like the job I thought I would have when I went to

138

the city. That was a dream, but it became a nightmare. I think it's worth hearing him out."

His tone sends a chill. "Not when you have no plans to go back."

"Do you want to go with me Monday so you can hear what he has to say?"

He jerks the fishing pole out of the ice. "You're going Monday?" He tosses the gear onto the ice next to the four-wheeler. "You said yes before talking to me?"

The hair rises on the back of my neck. "I didn't know I needed permission."

He stands and folds his chair. "I think it's time to pack up."

"Wayne, I don't understand. I'm only going for lunch and to listen. There's no signed contract or moving truck or anything."

He faces me, arms folded against his chest. "I don't think you get it. By meeting with this guy, you're saying you are open to the idea. If you had no plans to leave Speculator Falls, you wouldn't want to see what he has to say."

I shake my head and pack my things onto the back. "That's your interpretation, not mine."

"It's pretty straightforward. If you have no desire to leave the area, don't go Monday."

Wayne starts the ATV, a relief so I don't have to answer. The air remains still as we pack the gear and tie it onto the back. Holding on isn't as dreamy as he seems to find every bump on the lake. By the time we reach his house, the silence is as thick as the ice we drove over.

"I think I owe Aiden the chance to talk."

He digs his keys out of his pocket. "You've already heard him talk about the changes."

An impasse forms as Wayne struts to his front door and I march to my car. Hot tears threaten to form. "What happens if I go?"

Wayne shrugs. "I'm not giving an ultimatum, Trish. You've worked hard to change your reputation. Remember how we met? Shirley harassed you for leaving town."

"But it's not like that. I'm not leaving."

"If you go to that lunch, it sends a message."

I sigh and unlock my car before facing him. "You're welcome to come with me. I wish you would."

He turns away to unlock his door. I wait for his reply. It opens and he walks inside, closes the entrance behind him, and leaves me alone.

# Chapter Twenty-Three

The blinking light on my car charger doesn't lie. My phone isn't dead, but apparently communications with Wayne are. The longer I'm on Route 12 South, destination Binghamton, the harder the realization hits.

My luncheon with Aiden could be the end of Wayne and me.

I breathe slow and consider calling him. Fear of rejection and the memory of Wayne at church returning questions with one-word answers nix the idea. Turning the radio up is an option to drown out my thought, but no song can play loud enough.

*Lord, it's You I need. I don't think I'm wrong to hear what Aiden has to say. But Wayne's upset and I'm scared. Help me.*

I return the volume to normal as if God's going to speak out loud to me. The final forty-five minute drive reveals nothing but music. When I park at the restaurant and look for Aiden, my emotions bob and weave like a boxer in a prizefight. Aiden stands at the booth and waves.

There's no turning back.

Aiden shakes my hand and helps me with my coat. "Trish, it's great to see you. Did you have a good drive?"

I run my hand through the back of my hair and sit across from him. "I did, thanks. I forget once I leave the mountains that we're the only place with a lot of snow." I pick up the menu. "So, how are you? You look, refreshed. Not stressed."

He nods, and a sandy blond strand of hair bounces. "It's true. The new CEO has a completely different approach than anything I've ever seen. He wants employees to be visually stimulated and motivated. They bought property on Long Island. The plan is to have one campus with all employees there. Cubicles are gone. The new offices will be smaller, but Sam Cipher, the CEO, wants open spaces. Art throughout the interior. Comfy seating for meetings. Cafes. Walking paths. Tables outside with landscaping and ponds. I could go on and on."

That's certainly not a corporate concept I'm used to.

"You won't be based in Manhattan?"

Aiden shakes his head. "Crazy, right? I've seen the blueprints. It's going to be amazing. Sam doesn't even have an office in our current building. He wants to be accessible."

I rest my arms on the table. "Wow. A lot has changed."

We order, but after drinks arrive, Aiden stays on topic. "When clients come in for recruiting or training, my department creates all events while they are meeting with us. Orientations. Team-building exercises. Mixers. Goal celebrations. Whether it's bagels in the morning or an all-out blowout, I'm in charge of it all."

These happenings are everything I thought I'd be doing when I accepted the job. "That's fantastic. How big is your team?"

His smile widens. "Twelve. Sam wants to expand it. I could have as many as twenty. We have twice the clients we did when you were there, with more potential business."

The more he talks, the more energy fills our booth. When our food arrives, it's like a magnetic force surrounds us, making it impossible to ignore his excitement. And the opportunity that I could have it, too.

After a few bites of his marinated chicken on the fresh baked submarine roll, he clears his throat. "Trish, I didn't drive two and a half hours to tell you how great my life is. I have an immediate opening now, and I want you to take it."

My ice water goes down wrong and I cough hard enough that other patrons look over. "Sorry. Wrong pipe." I wave my napkin before dabbing the edges of my mouth, then focus on Aiden. "What is it? On the phone you said something about partner?"

He picks at a French fry. "That was my hope, but they want to wait a year for that. You would be on my team. Pitching ideas for different themed events. Writing purchase orders. Setting up. Picking folks up from airports. Creating team exercises. Some of it on your own, most of it with the rest of the group."

Okay, not partner. Still, a big improvement over what work they gave me last time I was in the city. "What's the potential for advancement?"

"As soon as I get the go-ahead for partner, I would want it to be you."

*Is my breathing shallow? Are my hands perspiring? Is this excitement or a panic attack?*

"I appreciate your confidence. However, it took me a while to recover from being let go. I feel like I'm finally getting some career traction."

He glances at his phone. "Didn't you e-mail me that you work at a department store?"

"It's my mom's business. I help out. I meant the Greater Adirondack Chamber of Commerce. I'm trying to create a position there, and the feedback has been very positive."

"Let's zero in on this. How much money are you making? Wait. Don't answer that, I'm not supposed to ask, and, I need to show you something." He reaches inside his coat and produces a pen. After a few scribbles on the napkin, he slides the paper to me. "Because this is what you'd start at."

My pulse races at the figure.

Aiden crosses the numbers out and replaces them with a new amount. "This is what you'd make if you were my partner."

"I don't know what to say."

He looks to his phone again and takes a drink of water. "Well, I do. Say yes. You wanted events planning, Trish. This is the job."

I fidget with the napkin. "When do you need an answer?"

He chuckles, taking out his wallet. "I was hoping to have one before I drive back."

Now it's my turn to laugh. "Aiden, I need time to think it over. I'm seeing someone, and it's kind of serious. He has a son, and then there's my mom and the store, and my portfolio…"

Aiden places his credit card on top of the bill as the waitress picks them up. "I understand. Is a week long enough?"

Ugh. I was hoping for two. Or a month. "Sure. Thanks for everything. I appreciate the offer, and that you drove all the way here."

"Same here. Looks like you have a lot to think about as you head back to snow country."

⌛⌛⌛

Four hours later, I'm back in Speculator Falls with a headache and cramped hands from gripping the steering wheel. Aiden's words fill my mind and I can't resist thinking about my future being on his team. Yet, after changing to jeans and a sweater and re-applying my makeup, I also want to see Wayne.

I take a chance and drive to his house where his truck sits in the driveway and the lights are on in the living room. My heart feels like it's pounding through my toes as I inch toward the front door. I ring the bell once and hear footsteps.

His calming blue eyes nearly make me forget why I'm there. "Trish. Hey."

I try to smile but I feel so numb I wonder if this is what it feels like to get Botox. "Hi. Can I come in?"

He swings the door open and gestures me to enter. "Do you want coffee? Cocoa?"

"No, thanks. I want to talk. We promised early on we'd be honest with each other."

Wayne pales and reaches for the arm of his chair to steady himself. "We did. What's going on? I take it you went to Binghamton."

I sit across from him on the couch, legs trembling. "Yeah. Aiden offered me a job. The company isn't the same as when I worked there. They've made a lot of improvements, including their location. The vision they have is what I wanted all along. It's in events planning and I would be part of a team."

144

His expression turns to granite.

"The salary is a twenty percent raise from what I made when I worked there before, and obviously more than my current pay."

He draws in a deep breath and blows out a long sigh. "This is exactly what I thought would happen."

My eyebrows arch and my stomach clenches. "What do you mean?"

"You said you wanted to go to hear him out. Now, you're interested. I can see it in your eyes."

I narrow my gaze. "It's a great opportunity and a blessing he wants me for it."

Wayne looks to the floor before focusing on me. "Is it enough to be asked?"

"I don't understand."

"Trish, did you leave that meeting with a boost of confidence, a redemption of sorts that gives you peace to pursue your future here? Or, did you drive home considering his offer?"

His question sucks the air out of me. I close my eyes and shake my head. "I don't know."

He moves to the couch, facing me. Our knees touch, and the electricity between us could light up the village. "I think you do."

"Maybe both. When I was let go, it killed my confidence. I was left with nothing. It felt good to hear I was needed. But, the position is everything I studied for, wanted. I'm torn."

There's nothing but a clock tick for several moments.

Wayne's voice is soft, his tone, calm. Too calm. "I love you, Trish. I'm happy that someone sees in you what I always have."

I swallow hard. "But…"

He slowly nods. "As much as I love you, I have to consider Noah. Before Aiden contacted you, we were planning a future that would unite the three of us. You were starting a career that would keep you local. Noah traveled with you to help because he wanted to get to know you better."

My lips quiver as tears form. "I know."

"You were spending time with him to see how you two got along, knowing the end goal was for you to be his step-mom."

Blinking only makes the tears fall faster. "I know."

Wayne stands and brushes the side of his hand against his cheek. "You're allowed to be torn. I know you aren't feeling this way on purpose to destroy us. But, we're at a place that puts our future in question."

Bile rises up and I will it back down. *Please don't say what I think you're going to say.*

"Trish, Noah doesn't deserve to be hurt. If you aren't absolutely positive about staying in town and creating a future with us, I have to protect him."

"What are you saying?"

"I think we need to press pause on us until you make a decision about your future."

# Chapter Twenty-Four

Jenna plants a caramel latte next to the department store register and takes a sip out of her travel cup. "Don't worry, it's caffeine free. Baby's fine." She pushes my drink closer to me. "But the question is, how are you?"

I grip the protective sleeve. "You're a good friend. Since Wayne told me we're pressing pause, you've checked on me every day."

She narrows her gaze. "You didn't answer my question."

Pregnancy only enhances her sass.

"It's been a few days and I volley back and forth with emotions. Confused. Sad. Angry. I don't know what pause means. Are we done? Do we stop dating, but stay in touch? I don't understand."

Jenna sips. "Have you tried to call? Text?"

I glance at my phone on the other side of the register. "I start to, then chicken out. Everything feels out of sorts. That lunch was unofficial. I learned about the job, that Aiden wants me to have it, but there was no paperwork. I liked what he had to say. I'm interested, but it hasn't been offered. Am I losing Wayne over nothing?"

She sighs and picks up a souvenir pen, and taps it. "I think you need to reach out to Wayne and say that to him."

"You're right. I need to explain what the job description is, the responsibility, and why I think it is important to my career. Make a list or something about the job." I glance at the clock. "Do you have to get back to the senior center?"

Jenna shakes her head. "I have some time. Shirley's got it under control."

I reach under the counter and pull out a legal pad. "It's not busy here. Want to help me create a list?"

She looks around the store before returning her attention to me. "Can I grab the camp chair? My feet are a little swollen."

I jog over and pick up the folding seat, setting it up for her. "Can you write things down while I think out loud?"

She waves the Adirondack pen. "On it. I've got a column marked what's real, and what's a feeling."

I draw in a deep breath and slowly let the air out like a child with a balloon. "I feel like the job is a second chance at something I went to school for and thought I'd enjoy."

Jenna scribbles. "But, the reality is, nothing was officially offered to you."

I nod. "I feel like I could have the opportunity to join an established business as opposed to starting from scratch here with my proposal for the Greater Adirondack Chamber." I take a drink from my lukewarm beverage. "I have Aiden's support, but no idea about how his bosses feel. As far as the Chamber, Ed Sterling was impressed with me at Christmas, and I've built my portfolio since then. The truth is, I have a decent chance at receiving chamber approval."

She looks up from the legal pad. "The reality is New York City living wasn't what you expected."

Images of the rat in my apartment come to mind, and there's no way to make that glamourous. "And as much as I dreaded coming back, I finally find life in Speculator Falls charming. I enjoy living here."

Her pen scratching against the paper is the only sound for a moment. "Time to add Wayne to the list. The reality is you were making plans for the future. Serious enough that he wanted you to consider the role you would have as a step-mom."

Noah's mess of curls comes to mind with that dimpled smile of his. "There's no way I can be present in their lives if I'm in New York City."

Jenna tosses the writing utensils on the floor. "That's your bottom line. Trish, how much do you love Wayne? If you can't live without him, then the job offer, if it comes, isn't worth it. If you don't feel deeply committed to him and Noah, then that pause needs to change to a stop."

I bury my face in my hands for a moment. "You're absolutely right. You've given me so much to pray about. Can I get a moon cookie for you as thanks?"

She struggles with rising from the folded chair and standing, that cute belly of hers revealing her second trimester status. "No, I appreciate it though. It's a blessing we can share. I look back to how we first met---not great friendship potential. I love what God's done between us." Jenna hobbles over and gives a quick hug.

"You've been one of the best parts of moving back here. After work I'll stop by the health center and see if Wayne's available to talk. I'll pour my heart out to him and let God take care of the rest."

⧗⧗⧗

The cruel March winds slap at my face and steal my breath as I leave work and drive the quarter mile to the health center. Wayne's SUV is in the lot, so I park and take a deep breath. *Father God, help me say the right things. I know he's my future. Help me tell him that.*

The bell above the door jingles as I gently press on the entrance and saunter over to the reception desk. No one is there, or the small waiting area. Carrie Underwood's latest hit filters through the speakers and seems to be the only activity in the room.

I step into the hallway that leads to patient care. "Wayne? Hello?"

A high-pitched laugh fills the hallway. Definitely not Wayne's. I shuffle a few more paces. "Hi, is Wayne back there?"

The fun grows louder with a male hoot in sync with the female. I turn the corner and see Wayne standing behind Jill, arms wrapped around her front. Still giggling, Jill turns around, and now they are facing each other, inches apart.

My keys slip from my hands and clang on the cement floor. I reach down for them, ready to flee as fast as possible, a sick twisting inside that's probably my intestines wrapping in a knot.

Wayne releases Jill and approaches the hallway. "Trish?"

Waves of hurt jumble my stomach as I stand with a death-grip on my keys. "Hey. I didn't mean to interrupt."

He turns to Jill, then back to me. "It isn't how it looks."

I shake my head. "I guess I understand what pause means now."

Jill's tone turns sultry as she beckons for Wayne. "Come back, I haven't finished."

I am so done here.

Wayne reaches for my wrist, but I push it away, my voice shaky. "I'm sorry. I have to go."

He follows me. "Trish, wait."

I refuse to look back as I push hard on the door, sending the bell into a frenzy. I don't hear footsteps as I rush out and unlock my car. Only when I'm in the driver's seat do I dare search for him.

He didn't follow.

# Chapter Twenty-Five

Three times I place a colored pencil on a blank page in my sketchbook only to lift it up and create nothing. Not even a dot. This has been my routine for days.

Dad strolls into the living room and pats my shoulder. "Trish, Mom called for dinner five minutes ago. Are you coming?"

I drop the would-be art onto the coffee table. "Sorry, I got distracted."

He walks over and sits on the couch. "Are you working on your storefront ideas?"

A sad laugh escapes. "Trying to."

Dad nods. "Hear anything from Aiden?"

I shake my head. "No. Not yet."

He nods. "Waiting's hard, isn't it?"

I tighten my ponytail. "Yeah. So much is up in the air. Whether I'll be recruiting more window work though the Greater Chamber. If an official job offer will materialize with Aiden." I was drained just sharing it. "And then there's Wayne."

Dad extends his hand and helps me stand. "I haven't seen him around. Everything okay?"

We head toward the dining room, my shoulders heavy with burden. "We weren't in agreement about my lunch with Aiden. Then, I caught him in a compromising position with his coworker."

He starts to speak, but I shake my head and take a seat. I've re-played the scene until I fall asleep. The week feels like a clock on a dying battery. Nothing moves forward. At the very least, I want to enjoy a good dinner.

Mom smiles as I reach for the ladle and scoop some beef stew. "I made bread today, it's still warm." She holds the bowl of meat and potatoes I pass to her. "You look thin. You could eat a little more."

Is this her way of asking what's going on between Wayne and me?

"I don't know about that, but I love your bread. I'll definitely have a couple slices."

We chew in silence for a few moments, but I notice Mom glancing over my way more than once. She's fidgeting in her chair and folding her napkin like it's an origami project.

I clear my throat and focus on her. "Everything okay, Mom?"

She pats the napkin and pushes it aside. "I guess I have a lot on my mind. Things are moving along with your father's work. I'm thinking about the store, especially if you move again. Then there's Wayne…"

Dad shoots her a stare filled with enough blinking to be a Morse code message.

I put my fork down. "Mom, I have a lot on my mind, too. There's so much to sort out, and what I saw with Wayne is hard to unsee. I don't think we have the future I'd expected."

Mom pours herself a glass of ice water. "Did you let him explain? I know that Jill girl is known as a troublemaker."

She sure is. "I left before he could, and I haven't heard from him. He didn't let me explain why meeting with Aiden was so important to me. He assumed I was moving because I had one call."

Dad clears his throat. "Well? Are you moving?"

Is a shrug an acceptable reply?

"Jay, I think Trish should talk to Wayne so they can sort things out."

Dad sighs, the kind I remember hearing after he got off a long work call with a difficult client. "Honey, Trish is an adult and so is Wayne. Whatever they need to work out, I have faith they will."

Nothing like talking about me as if I'm not even in the room. "You have a good idea, Dad. Faith. I do need to sort things out with Wayne. As nervous as I am about what he might say, church is the best place to have that conversation."

Before anyone can mention me in third person, my phone buzzes. I excuse myself and look at the screen to learn its Aiden Parker. "I need to take this." I scurry to my room for privacy.

"Trish, hey. Thought I'd tell you the latest. I talked to my boss and his boss gave us the green light for a few positions for my team."

My heart starts pounding as I pick at a hangnail. "That's great. Is it the position we talked about?"

"It isn't. That's why I'm calling. I had it in my head that I'd have a partner, a co-lead, and I wanted you. They want to see how I manage a team on my own for a while. They are looking for me to find team members. Many of the same duties as a team lead for events planning."

I roll my eyes. "But more of the errand running and less pay."

"My goal would be to make sure the team works together in planning and executing events. Not just the mundane running around on the day of an activity. I'm holding interviews next week downtown. Interested? I could even take you to the new campus for a tour."

"I don't know, Aiden. It sounds a lot like the job I lost."

"One difference. I have the ability to select who to promote. An interview isn't a blood covenant. Please say yes."

I close my eyes and see Wayne holding Jill. Our last time together when he told me we needed to press pause. I can't reach for any recent happy moments between us. "Okay, you're right. There's no harm in going to the interview. I'll go."

Aiden wastes no time. "Great. You'll get an email this week with all the information. It will be from me and my boss. Glad we talked, Trish. See you next week."

With phone in hand, I barely end the call before it rings again. "What did you forget, Aiden?"

A deep voice speaks, and I instantly realize it's not my potential boss from New York City. "Miss Maxwell?"

"Hello? Speaking."

"It's Ed Sterling from the Greater Adirondack Chamber of Commerce. Do you have a few minutes to talk?"

☒☒☒

Sunday service seems long because I know I have to reach out to Wayne and see where we stand. Tell him about my interview with Aiden. That Ed Sterling wants me to return to show my new portfolio. These are things to tell a best friend, and my heart hurts that there's distance between me and Wayne.

I dodge Dora Parks mid-aisle at dismissal as I observe Wayne heading toward the lobby. Shirley greets me with a hello, and I return the gesture with a smile as I jog into the foyer area. Wayne's ten feet away, talking with Pastor Reynolds and Brooke.

Pastor's the first to see me approach. "Trish, how lovely to see you. I feel like we haven't talked with you for a long time."

I position myself next to Wayne, but not too close. "It has been busy. Thank you for a great message today. I needed the reminder of what my real treasures are." I glance at Wayne.

He runs a hand through his curls and bites his lip.

Brooke tugs on her husband's sleeve. "There's Shirley. We were going to talk to her about that thing."

Pastor furrows his brow and is about to speak, but Brooke waves him on and he starts to turn. "Good seeing you, Wayne, Trish. Have a blessed week."

I start talking before Wayne can leave. "We need to talk. A lot is going on. I miss you."

He looks to the floor. "A different response than a few days ago when you wouldn't let me talk to you."

I nod. "I know, and I'm sorry. Can we go somewhere to talk? Please?"

"It's cool, but sunny. Want to grab a picnic table near the beach?"

Twenty minutes and a basket full of food later, we park across the street and walk side-by-side to the grassy area next to the beach.

154

Wayne sits at the table closest to the steps that lead down to the sand, sunglasses on. His navy windbreaker flaps in the steady breeze.

I can't stop staring at how handsome he is. "You look good. As usual."

His sunglasses won't let me see any physical response. "So do you. What's this about? That night with Jill?"

"I jumped to conclusions and let my frustrations get in the way. I'm sorry."

He keeps an even, calm tone. "She's my partner for the time being. Boss switched her away from Brad. We were arguing about the Heimlich maneuver. I was showing her the correct way to administer it."

I learned that in elementary school. Jill has to know it, too. "Did you think perhaps she was putting a move on you?"

He traces his finger against the wood grain. "Yes, but in case she was telling the truth, I thought I should show her. Chances are she will have a choking victim while on duty someday."

Good point. "I also wanted to tell you about my career stuff. Things are happening, and I hate that you aren't a part of it. Maybe that's what the 'press pause' status means for us."

Wayne clears his throat. "Trish, I have to look out for the future. I want you in it, so does Noah. But if you're wavering about where you'll be, I have to protect my family. I've missed you so much. You have no idea how many times I wanted to pick up the phone, or stop at the store to see you."

My hand moves across the table to find his. "I know. I would never intentionally hurt either of you. I'm curious is all. I want God to show me what's next. Working at the department store isn't something I see long-term."

He squeezes and holds on. "What do you see? Where are you? Here? New York City?"

Fear seizes my throat. "I don't know. But we promised honesty."

Wayne doesn't let up with his gaze. "You're going to New York."

I nod. "For an interview. It isn't official. Nothing is."

He loosens the grip. "But it sends the same message. That you aren't content here and that Noah and I aren't enough."

I can't shake my head fast enough. "I also am meeting with Ed Sterling again. He called me. He wants to see my updated portfolio. I'm exploring all my options."

He breathes in deep, and is slow to exhale. "I love you, Trish. I've never felt like this before."

"But?"

"But, I have to guard my heart and Noah's. It doesn't mean I don't love you, and it sure doesn't give Jill any chance to manipulate me."

I realize I'm holding my breath, and that his hand isn't holding mine.

"Until you know what you want and where you want it, I have to keep my distance. I can't process why you even want to go to New York if you feel you have a future with me."

# Chapter Twenty-Six

March transitions to April. My interview with Aiden Parker in Manhattan bleeds into my appointment with Ed Sterling in Saranac Lake. Hundreds of miles apart, and two completely different career paths. Yet, both said they would call with information. Like a high school girl hoping for a date, I'm waiting for the phone to ring.

Thankfully, the store keeps me busy. One morning while unloading my first summer shipment, the bell chimes and I glance at the front entrance. It's Noah, and I swallow hard. I miss him.

He saunters over to the jewelry section, peeking in my direction every minute or so.

Do I go over? Say something?

Noah holds up a charm bracelet. "Would a girl my age like this?"

I stroll over as if I know exactly what I'm doing and what I'm going to say. This teen has my heart as much as his dad does. "Hi to you, too." I pick up the other end of the bracelet and admire the fairytale themed charms. "Ah, this is a popular one. Most girls I know love this one because it reminds them of their favorite princess movies."

He rolls this eyes. "Too girlie for me. But I see the slipper. And the mirror."

I nod and point to another charm. "There's a book. A frog wearing a crown. A teapot. It really is nice. Is this for Alyssa?"

Noah shakes his head. "That's over. It's for Olivia. She's kind of going through some stuff and I thought this might cheer her up." He turns it over and looks at the price tag. "Ouch. There goes my allowance money."

I bite my lip for a moment. "I can give you my discount. Don't worry about it."

His crooked grin warms me from head to toe. "Thanks, Trish. Do you wrap?"

I hope this Olivia knows what a great kid Noah is. "I do. I'll make sure it's fit for a princess."

We amble to the counter and I find a box under the register. When I start to wrap, Noah takes out his wallet and pulls out wrinkled bills.

"So, is Olivia a girlfriend?"

Noah shrugs and fidgets with his money. "Not yet."

He gets his charm from his dad.

I reach for some pink ribbon and measure it out. "She'd be a fool not to like you."

"Thanks. Trish, I wish you and my dad were still together."

The scissors feel like a ball of lead as my heartbeat accelerates at Wayne's mention. "We're still friends. It's complicated."

He pushes the payment toward me. "I disagree. You two were super happy together. Dad told me you guys are in limbo because you don't know what you want."

Pangs of loneliness give me an ache inside. "We both want the best for everyone, most of all, you. I had an interview downstate. It has a lot of appeal. So does the work you and I did at the library when you were on break. Both jobs would make me feel needed."

"My dad needs you."

My knees nearly buckle with his piercing gaze and confession. "Noah. I miss him and you so much. Every time your dad and I talk, we can't agree."

"He thinks you'll get the job in New York City and leave us."

This kid pulls no punches, and I feel battered.

"I'm curious about it. My first time there was a disaster. It would be nice to at least hear the company wants me back. I don't think I'd leave Speculator Falls, but that's not enough for your dad."

He nods. "If they offer you that position, I don't see you taking it."

I give him his small change back, along with the wrapped box. "What makes you say that?"

Noah shrugs. "You aren't a little fish in a big pond here. The Trish I know lights up Speculator Falls at Christmas. For real. You create those displays for small businesses. Work with the senior center. Help your family here. No big company is going to notice you like all of us have."

The kid's honesty knocks the wind out of me. "Thanks, Noah. Um, I'll be praying for Olivia."

Noah stuffs the change in his pocket, reaches for the box, and heads for the door. As the bell jingles, he stops. "I'm praying for you and dad."

⧖⧖⧖

Even after the weeks of separation between Wayne and me, it's still awkward to enter the church sanctuary and not sit by him. This Sunday's no different as I force a smile and a wave as I walk by his pew and join my parents.

Dad moves over and pats my back. "Pastor Reynolds is announcing my retirement today."

Wow, this is happening. Everything is lining up for Mom and Dad.

"That's great. Will you two join the senior center?" I can't picture the two of them in the variety show or playing cards.

He chuckles and looks to Mom, and then me. "We might. Work was always in the way, but we'd like to do some gardening. Take some day trips."

Mom sighs. "The house needs a deep cleaning. I suppose we should conquer that."

Before I can respond, Pastor steps up to the platform. "Good morning! Anyone see the tulips starting to bloom? What a beautiful sight. Before we start worship, I thought I'd highlight a couple items from the bulletin."

I pick up mine and open it, noticing everyone around me does the same.

"First, Jay Maxwell is handing over the keys to his law practice on July third. I know that's a couple months away, but save the date.

We definitely as a church family want to celebrate with him, so stay tuned."

Fred Beebe leans forward and taps Dad on the shoulder. "You'll love retirement, and you'll be busier than you ever were. It's the craziest thing."

Dad grins. "No thank you. I'm ready to slow the pace a little."

Pastor folds the bulletin and turns it over. "The health center is offering a CPR class here on Tuesday, and Wayne Peterson is our instructor. This is a great class for anyone, especially our leaders. I pray we never have to use the technique on anyone, but it's important to know. Now, let's have the praise team start a wonderful time of worship."

The mention of Wayne's name seems to open the cage of butterflies in my stomach. I turn to steal a glance, and realize he's looking in my direction. His royal blue shirt enhances those kind eyes. I hope the sermon is on self-control, because I have none.

When it's time for Pastor to deliver the message, he places his well-worn Bible on the wooden pulpit. "Have you ever tried to lead an activity with someone who doesn't want to listen to directions? Our oldest is a student teacher in elementary school and he told us about a young man who decided to make a craft before hearing how to put it together. It was only after the boy finished he held up the mangled mess and asked if he did it right. Anyone relate to the frustration?"

Heads nod and murmurs pop up across the sanctuary.

"That's what today's message is about. Trusting God with life's directions."

Those anxious butterflies spread from head to toe.

"The Book of Joshua starts off with instructions from God. Joshua needs to pay attention because the Israelites didn't listen to Moses, and the people paid a hefty price. But this is a new generation, and they're willing to obey. I'm sure there was fear, that they heard the stories from their ancestors. They had no proof they'd find the Promised Land in their lifetime."

Was New York City my Promised Land? Not so long ago I thought so.

Pastor Reynolds opens his Bible. "And even if they made it, there were threats from other nations. If I were Joshua, my plan would have been to freeze. Because the past was scary, and so was the future."

Oh, Joshua, I get you.

"But the leader acted in wisdom. He waited for God's orders instead of trying to make it happen. The first order, don't paralyze yourself. Joshua didn't plant his feet in cement, and neither should we. Not knowing what's ahead can cause us to stay put. Do nothing. Ignore His voice. Another command is one I'm guilty of, don't presume. I'm always trying to second guess what God's up to. I should wait and listen, but I'm usually asking Him and everyone else so many questions."

I look over and see Mom scribbling away. Should I be taking notes?

"Let's turn to Proverbs 16:9." He waits a moment. "In his heart a man plans his course, but the Lord determines his steps. Here are the instructions. Don't paralyze yourself. Don't presume. Sarah went ahead of God's plan and it didn't go well for her. So, what to do? Pray. I don't mean a quick, 'Help!' I am challenging all of us to seek Him with everything you've got. Fast. Talk to Him in the car. The shower. In private moments at home. But know He hears us. And He cares."

Suddenly, I feel like those butterflies are tamed and back in the cage.

I don't hear the rest of the message. I never thought about God caring what happens next with me. I've been too busy asking and pushing my way into my future. When Pastor asks if anyone wants to pray, I kneel right where I am.

"Lord, I've been more like the Israelites Moses was leading, and I want to be Joshua. Help me seek You more than the approval of others. Forgive me for wandering in circles."

When I rise a few minutes later, I notice the altar is full of praying people. Even Kyle Swarthmore is up front with Pastor Reynolds. I'm the only one in the pew. But Wayne is heading my way.

His smile is nearly my undoing. "Hi, Trish. Good message, right?"

"It was just what I needed to hear. Wayne, I don't know what God's plan for me is. But I'm ready to let Him show me."

His beam warms me from head to toe. "Have you heard from the Chamber?"

Our hands touch on the pew, and a surge of electricity courses up my spine. "No. I haven't heard from anyone. Both Ed and Aiden said no matter what the answer was, it would take a couple weeks."

He nods and inches his hand closer to mine. "Did you want to pray together?"

"I'd love that."

Wayne laces his fingers with mine. "God, we look to You as the author and finisher of all things, including Trish's future. You know what's best for her. You know I love her. Help her, help us trust You to make our paths straight. We thank You in advance, and it's for Your glory. Amen."

I don't let go. "Amen."

He swings our hands. "So, do you have plans for this afternoon?"

# Chapter Twenty-Seven

Wayne takes a sip of his ice water and pushes the Jack Frosty's menu to the side. "I've missed you, Trish. I want to work this out."

I recall part of the sermon. Remember God orders our steps. He knows. "I do, too. We have to trust God through the job and relationship process. I worked with Jenna on a list about each job, and I think something about New York City came to light that I didn't realize before."

He pales. "I'm starting to hate the words 'New York City.'"

"I understand, but it isn't what you think. Jenna and I wrote things out and an aspect of the job with Aiden is that I get a second chance. I went there thinking I was going to change the world and show everyone in Speculator Falls. Instead, I returned here humiliated with a lot of apologies to make. I was certain my life was going to be glamorous and metropolitan, filled with event planning. I guess I want to hear a 'yes' from them so I won't feel like I was wrong."

Wayne clears his throat. "How far do you have to carry that need to feel fulfilled by a dream that was crushed? Will Aiden offering the job officially be enough? Do you need to rent an overpriced, rat- infested apartment before you feel redeemed? That's what I don't understand."

I nod, because he's not wrong. "I'm hoping the call will be enough."

"And if it isn't?"

"We always said we'd be honest. The other revelation I had is the window display job. If the Greater Adirondack Chamber board feels I'm a good fit for their support, I'd still have to raise my own funding. They would promote me across the Adirondacks, make businesses aware I'm there to help them, but I'd have to have resources ready for each job."

He plays with the menu until our waitress takes the order. "You'd be like a missionary."

I furrow my brow. "In what way?"

"They have to raise their budget. You also would be traveling a lot, but it still would be within the Adirondacks. You could be based in Speculator Falls."

My thoughts drift to a future where Wayne and I are married. Living in the same home. Raising Noah. Even if the job is unstable, my overall life as I dream it feels secure.

Wayne's snapping fingers bring me back to reality. "Trish. You okay? Did you hear what I just said?"

Our food arrives, and I try to recall his words. "I'm sorry, I was daydreaming."

The crease in his forehead tightens. "I know you're afraid of starting a job from nothing. But you wouldn't be alone. We would be a family."

My sigh could fill a bunch of balloons. "And if I moved to The Big Apple, I would be on my own."

Wayne picks up his fork. "You're making it seem like a threat. By your own words you've said all New York is to you is validation. We love each other. We want to be together. I don't get why this is so hard."

Suddenly, I'm not hungry, and I'm forgetting the sermon. "I don't want to fail."

His reply is a hoarse whisper. "Again."

The hair rises on the back of my neck. "What did you say?"

Wayne puts the fork down. "I corrected you. You're afraid of failing again."

I grab my purse and stand. "How could you say such a thing?"

"Trish, sit down. Let me explain."

I choke out the words. "What? All the ways I'm a failure? I'm sorry, I can't do this." I turn and march out the door, passing Jill, who is on her way in. "Go ahead, you can have him."

⌛⌛⌛

Two days later, I'm still grieving about the way things ended with Wayne as I drive to Schroon Lake. The more Wayne and I try to make our relationship work, the wider the chasm between us. My fifty mile commute north helps me clear my mind and pray as I prepare to create displays for the rural businesses.

"Father God, I'm confused and hurting. I don't understand why You would give Wayne and me such powerful feelings for each other when we can't seem to agree. I don't want him or Noah to have regrets, but this aches. Help me know what to do. Give me this time away from home to hear from You. Let praise and trust flow from me. Even if it doesn't work out the way I want. Amen."

I repeat similar prayers throughout my time at the credit union where I set up for a customized display. The wire roll I unpack reminds me of fishing line and my ice excursion with Wayne. I brush away fresh tears when a woman calls my name.

I drop the cable and turn. "Meg Anderson? What are you doing here?"

Jenna's younger sister stops in front of me. Her multi colored leggings enliven the drab foyer I hope to transform. "I go where the teaching jobs are. This one should take me to the end of the school year. I'm taking the place of a middle school Science teacher on maternity leave."

Pushing past a cramp in my leg, I rise and face her. "That's great. Maybe it will help you find something more permanent."

She shrugs. "Steady employment in this field is harder to come by than in Ohio. Kyle offered to float my resume around New Jersey, but I don't know. I really like this area, and with Jenna's baby, I don't want to move."

Meg's eyes sparkle as she mentions Kyle, and Jenna's bundle of joy.

"Sounds like you and Kyle are going strong." Another pang rocks my heart.

She tucks a piece of hair behind her ear. "We're taking it a day at a time. He's not the guy you all know. He's changed."

I remember seeing him at the altar, definitely something I'd never seen before. "That's great. How does Jenna feel about it?"

Meg rolls her eyes. "She's protective. And hormonal. If Jenna could lock me up in the spare room, she'd do it." Meg sobers, and clears her throat. "How about you? I haven't seen you and Wayne sitting together at church for quite some time."

I wish the floor would open up and take me to some secret vault where I could hide. "Yeah. We're kind of at an impasse. I'm not sure it's going to work out."

She reaches for my arm. "Trish, I'm sorry. You two looked so happy. I hope things change for the better. Well, I should get in line before they close. Good to see you."

Meg gives my arm a squeeze, waves, and trots off to the teller line. Hard to believe the college grad from Ohio who threw herself at Will Marshall last year was serious about Kyle. Before I have a chance to process it, my phone rings.

The ID comes up Aiden Parker.

# Chapter Twenty-Eight

I stare at the screen for a few rings, as I try to calm my heart rate. *What if Aiden offers the job? What do I say? What if he doesn't? Will I be relieved?* I breathe in and exhale with a silent prayer. *Lord, I place my trust in You. I'm done leaning on my own understanding. I know you will direct my steps. Amen.*

Peace wraps around me like a favorite blanket. "Hello, Aiden."

"Trish. I wanted to apologize for taking so long to get back to you. There's a lot going on, but I'm finally able to share where things are with my team and the hiring process."

Here we go.

My voice has a slight shakiness to it. "What's going on?"

"As I had mentioned early on, my desire to have you on board was unofficial. I wasn't promised much beyond building the team. I was denied the opportunity to hire the co-lead position until next year. Your interview was for the position of team event associate."

I tap my foot at the same speed I would if I'd drank ten energy drinks. "Right. Just spill it, whatever it is."

A sigh from the other end greets me. "My boss thought your interview was strong, but he had someone in mind the entire time. He outranks me, so his niece is getting the position. I'm sorry. I believe there will be more openings very soon, and I'd like to consider you for one of them."

I freeze. New York City isn't the place for me. The revelation falls on me like a beautiful, gentle rain. I didn't need that job for redemption. I didn't get it as confirmation.

"Aiden, it's fine. I appreciate you taking the time to interview me. You can shred the resume."

He clears his throat. "Are you sure? Just because it's a no today doesn't mean it always will be."

The more peace I feel, the bigger my grin grows. The knots in my shoulder disappear. "I'm sure. I'm meant to stay in the Adirondacks."

And God willing, find my way back into Wayne's arms and future.

☒☒☒

Once I complete the Schroon Lake storefronts on Friday and add the work to my growing portfolio, I call Ed Sterling to see if they have any news concerning my position within the Greater Adirondack Chamber.

The administrative assistant's tone sounds like a deflating balloon. "I'm so sorry, you just missed him. He's not only gone for the day, he starts a two week vacation. I'll make sure he returns your call as soon as he's back."

Ugh. Hurry up and wait seems to be the theme for me.

By Saturday, my life's pace feels at a standstill, even with the peace I have about not getting the job with Aiden. With winter weather behind us in Speculator Falls, business should be picking up at the department store, but it's not very busy.

Of course, that's when Shirley McIlwain enters.

She doesn't even browse and pick up items like the last time. She marches right up to the counter and slams her purse down. "What's this I hear about you interviewing for a job in New York?"

The temperature in the room feels like it is rising to a volcanic level as beads of sweat form on my forehead and palms.

Shirley doesn't give me a moment to explain. "You've been down that road before. It didn't work. Remember?"

I open my mouth, but her narrow gaze paralyzes me.

"Trish Maxwell, you're an asset to this community. You belong in Speculator Falls. You always did. Get that through that beautiful head of yours."

Wait. What?

My temperature cools and I feel comfortable as I smile. "Shirley, that's the nicest thing you've ever said to me. Thank you."

She swats her hand as if she were hitting a fly. "Well, it's true."

I take the bold step to reach for her hand and squeeze it. "I didn't get the job. I think deep down I never wanted it. I wanted to feel like they needed me after they let me go. I love it here. I don't want to go."

Her grin widens. "Good for you. So, what's next? Taking over this store when your parents retire?"

My laugh echoes throughout the aisles. "No. When Dad's home full-time, I suspect Mom will be anxious to put more hours in here. I'll help out as they need me, but I believe I know the direction God's given me. I'm meant to be in the Adirondacks."

"Praise God. How does your paramedic feel about it?"

Just hearing about Wayne is a blow. "We aren't together."

Shirley rolls her eyes. "That's ridiculous. I watched Ben and Jenna battle back and forth before they finally got together. Life's too short. The man is in love with you, and I can see by the goofy look on your face that you feel the same. Go get him, Trish. What do you have to lose?"

"I hope to see him over the weekend."

Shirley nods. "See that you do. He's a keeper." She turns. "Now, I need a candle. Help me find something flowery that isn't going to make me gag."

Yes, Ma'am.

⧗⧗⧗

After church, I maneuver through the crowds with a repetitive "Excuse me," heading to the lobby in an effort to find Wayne. He darts out of the sanctuary and heads down the hall. Shirley's encouragement re-plays through my mind, and the sermon on bold faith gives me courage.

He's at a jogging pace as he moves toward the kitchen.

My high heels aren't going to let me reach him unless he slows down. "Wayne! Wait up."

Wayne turns, we lock eyes, and he stops. "Hey."

169

My bravery dissipates like fog on a summer morning. "Can we talk?"

There's no smile. His ocean blue eyes hold no sparkle. "Didn't we try that last week? It didn't end well."

I nod. "I know, and I'm sorry. I jumped to conclusions. I've been praying a lot and…"

He reaches for my elbow, sending a rush of electricity through my veins. "How about we move this somewhere more private. The kitchen should be free for ten more minutes."

He guides me inside the kitchen to the stainless steel counter. "You said you were praying."

My words spill out. "Wayne, you were right about not needing to pursue the job in New York City. I had to find out on my own. God showed me not receiving the offer was His confirmation. I belong here. Not there."

He places his hand on my shoulder. "That's great. God gave you direction you were seeking."

I take a step closer. "Now that I have it, you were the first I wanted to tell. We made it over that relationship hurdle. We can move forward and plan our future."

Wayne falls back a couple paces, sending my heart into a freefall. "Trish, when you insisted on going to Binghamton, I supported you even though I didn't agree. Then you were determined to interview in Manhattan, despite my misgivings. I felt you tossed my feelings aside. When we tried to talk it through after you returned, you bolted at the first sign of miscommunication."

The pit in my stomach evolves into an abyss. "I know. I messed up. I apologize."

"I forgive you. But…"

My hands shake in tandem with my voice. "Don't. Wayne, please."

He continues his retreat. "A successful relationship takes two people constantly working on unity. That's not us. Your journey might have helped you know what career path to pursue, but your methods pushed me completely out of the picture. Your actions separate us. I think it's best we make it permanent."

Engaged

Attending Jenna's baby shower is the last thing I want to do while I nurse a broken heart. Mom is applying her makeup when I beg her to go in my place.

She takes the mascara wand out of the tube. "Trish, Dad's transferring the law office over in six weeks. We have so much to do. You have the store under control. You can handle the party."

I want to hold my breath and stomp like I did as a toddler. "I'm not good company."

Mom holds still while she puts on her eye makeup. "That's your choice. Your father and I have tried to get you out of the house since your breakup. Jenna's called you. Instead, you mope around."

"It isn't moping. I'm afraid of missing Ed Sterling's call. I doubt my cell service would even work if he tried my number, so landline's his best bet."

She shoots me a narrow gaze. "I don't have time to argue, and neither do you."

Yeah, I'm not going to win this one.

An hour later I force myself to walk into the fellowship hall at the church. The place is decked out in gender neutral balloons and streamers. Carla stands at the entrance, and thankfully doesn't lose her smile when she sees me. "Hi, Trish. Thanks for coming."

"No problem. I appreciate being invited. My mom sends her apologies. She's at work with Dad."

Carla hands me a ticket and puts another in a baby bottle bank. "He's retiring soon, right?"

I nod and spot Jenna near the gift table. "Early July. They're transferring the practice over to a new lawyer in Syracuse. I hardly see them."

She rips another ticket. "They deserve a good retirement. You're also worthy of a happy ending. I hope you get it."

My jaw lowers. "Do you mean with work or Wayne?"

Carla winks. "Yes." She moves on to greet Ben's grandmother, Sara Bivins.

I take a deep breath and glance at my seating options. Most of the ladies from the senior center are already at tables. Shirley waves and calls out my name. "Trish, come on over!"

I know I'm the only Trish in town, but I want to turn around and see who she's talking to. Instead, I saunter over, raffle ticket and gift in hand. "Hi, everyone. Can you believe Jenna's almost ready to have the baby?"

Shirley's practically glowing. "We're so excited for her. She's going to be an excellent mom." She pulls out a chair. "Sit with us."

"Are you sure?"

She rolls her eyes as the other ladies coax me to join. "As certain as I am you and Wayne belong together."

Oh, boy. That's hard to interpret.

Once seated, I place a napkin on my lap and turn to Shirley. "Wayne and I broke up. For good."

She glances at the others, and they smile. "Trish, we know he dumped you. We also believe this story isn't over. Don't lose hope."

"That's sweet, but I don't see how. I hurt him and his trust in our future."

Retired realtor Mabel Coffey pours each of us a cup of ice water. "Honey, you did that to all of us when you left the senior center for that job. Now look. Here we all are, friends." She picks up her drink. "And ready to take guesses on whether Jenna has a boy or girl."

I sit with the group and enjoy catered food from Frosty's, and Carla's silly baby games. Jenna's all wrapped in toilet paper when her sister, Meg, announces it's almost time to eat cake. The mom-to-be ambles over to us.

Her breathing sounds like she climbed the mountain that is her driveway. "This table looks like a rowdy group of ladies."

I stand and give Jenna my seat. "I'm trying to keep them under control."

She giggles. "Funny, I had you pegged as the leader."

We all laugh, but Jenna sobers. "Trish, Meg told me she saw you a few weeks ago in Lake Schroon."

I look over to Meg, who is at the cake table with Carla. "Yes, it was nice to talk to her. She seems interested in making a life for herself here. That chat with her has helped me."

She nods, but her expression darkens. "Meg also seems insistent on making Kyle her entire agenda."

"He was at the altar talking with Pastor Reynolds a few weeks ago. That has to be good."

Carla's voice booms over the microphone. "Jenna, time to cut the cake."

Jenna pats my arm. "I hope so. I know I'm hormonal, but I can't get over the two of them together. I'm not sure I want to." She sighs. "That's a vent for another time. Let's have some chocolate."

Mabel speaks, but Jenna's already on her way to Carla. "Wait! We didn't get to find out if it was a boy or a girl."

The party wraps up after a good ninety minutes of unwrapping gifts. The senior center members blessed her with a crib, mattress, sheets, and the works. Jenna's family gave her a stroller and car seat. The smaller gifts like burp cloths and onesies were mostly yellows and greens since not even Jenna knows if they're having a boy or a girl. As I gather my raffle prize of a box of chocolates, Ben and Will enter the hall. Jenna greets her husband with a kiss. "I hope you both brought your trucks."

Ben raises his eyebrows. "That many gifts? Wow. Will's truck is at the shop."

Will steps forward. "I talked to Noah a bit ago. Wayne is off today. He can help. I'll text him."

Jenna's gaze is on me. "Is that okay?"

I pull keys out of my purse. "Oh, don't worry about me. I'm leaving." I look at the six boxes of diapers stacked in a corner. And the stroller, with gift bags piled on top. Then the high chair, with bibs, the crib mobile, wipes warmer and pacifiers. "Unless you need me."

She reaches over for an awkward hug. "Thank you."

Ben's truck and Jenna's car is full in fifteen minutes. When Wayne pulls in, we're starting to place gifts in Carla's SUV. My heartbeat rockets as soon as he saunters over to the parents-to-be.

Wayne chuckles. "Do you two need another house for all this?"

I retrieve my keys, hoping for a quick getaway.

Ben shakes his head. "We're blessed. I don't think there's an item left on the registry."

I side-step away from the vehicles to make my way to my car, but Wayne notices and can't keep silent.

"Hey, Trish. Looks like it was a fun party."

I stop, praying I can avoid his kind eyes. "It was great. It looks like everyone has everything under control, so I'm going."

The air is as still as when a storm's about to hit, but Wayne breaks the silence. "I hope you're doing okay. I've been thinking about you."

# Chapter Thirty

The day after her baby shower, I'm watching a cardinal visit Mom's feeder when Jenna calls.

"I'm having a moon cookie craving."

With Wayne's mixed messages and still no phone call from Ed Sterling, I'd eat a dozen of my favorite cookie if that's what she needs.

I turn from the patio and head back inside, in search of my keys. "Do you want me to grab a box?"

Jenna sighs. "Yes, but there's more. I'm being a pest, I know. I have to go to the hunting cabin, Sara left her favorite blanket and wants it back at her house. Do you mind getting the cookies? You could join me at the cabin."

I remember visiting the Bivins family home before building their current one. Calling it rustic is a generous description, and I hated going there when I dated Ben. "We aren't eating there, are we? Who knows how many hungry mice are waiting."

She laughs. "I'll probably have the package devoured before we even get to the paper trails."

An hour later, I pull in front of the breathtaking log home Ben and his late grandfather built. Jenna's waiting on the wrap-around porch with her face to the rare, summery feeling May sun.

Once I close my car door, with a box of cookies in my other hand, I amble towards her. "Sugar alert."

Jenna lowers her gaze and her smile brightens. "You're a lifesaver. Ben doesn't understand the cravings. I'm sick of vegetables." She punctures the wrapping with her nail and retrieves the sweet cookie iced with half-vanilla, half chocolate. "This is a need."

"It's been my go-to since I was ten. Ben's grandpa had them ready for me every time I came into JB's."

She gestures for me to follow her inside. "Let me get the keys to the ATV."

My mouth opens but no words come out. "Jenna, you can't be serious."

"What? You do remember trucks can't make it all the way to the hunting cabin, right?"

I nod. "Back when I dated Ben, we walked the last half mile. I thought that was your plan. You're having a baby next month. The last place you should be is on an ATV."

Jenna shrugs. "If it were muddy and full of ruts, I'd agree. It's flat. I'll drive slowly. Promise."

I can see Ben's tomato-colored face when he realizes I went ahead with her plan. "If you show any signs of labor, we turn around and go right to the hospital."

She rolls her eyes. "You worry too much. Let's put a couple cookies in a baggie for the road."

Well, that's one good idea she has.

With a five mile per hour pace, the ATV crawls to the cabin. Jenna's right about it not being bumpy, but the further we press into the woods, the darker it gets. With the sun playing peek-a-boo, I wish I brought my sweater.

Jenna stops in front of the cabin and turns off the machine. "We might need Sara's blanket to stay warm on the way back. It cooled down."

I look up at the sky and my throat constricts. The clouds aren't visible because the atmosphere is as black as charcoal and the air thick with mystery. "I hate to say it, but I think we need to snack inside. I don't think there's time to make it back to your house."

She furrows her brow. "You think it's going to storm? I won't melt with a little rain."

Ugh, the city-girl. "I don't think this is a gentle rain heading our way. I think we're going to get a decent thunderstorm. Find your cabin key and let's get in."

Jenna reaches in her pocket and produces the key. As soon as she jiggles the lock, a crack of thunder breaks the eerie silence in the sky. "That sounds close." The door opens, and she shuffles inside.

I follow, and the smell of must and pine invade my senses. It's so bleak outside that the lightning dances past the side window. "It is. I've been through a lot of storms with my parents. Listen to me and we'll be fine."

Her nod is slow and her hands shake as she grabs the blanket. "Okay. Ben's going to be furious with me."

Oh, that's an understatement, but we have bigger problems. Thunder and lightning bring on a third partner to their party---wind. Not a breeze, or even a gust. John Bivins told me years ago what a bad wind sounds like, and this freight train noise is it.

I close my eyes for a second. *Father, help us. Keep us safe. Be with the baby.* "Jenna, I'm moving the couch out, and you're going to bend down behind it."

The storm increases in strength and volume to the point we're shouting.

Jenna has tears rolling down her face. "I can't bend! I'm too big."

I race over to the couch and move it away from the wall, and then grab her wrist. "You have to try. Now!"

Once she's safely tucked behind the couch, I jump next to her and roll into a ball. Neither of us speak as the winds whip through the forest. I can't tell if the cracks are more thunder or trees falling, or both. I reach out for Jenna's hand and she squeezes so hard I wince, but it's the right thing to do.

The weather calms in probably twenty minutes, a fragment of light peeks through. I open my eyes and lift my head. Jenna's entire body shakes.

"It's okay. The worst is over." I remove my hand from hers and stand, offering her a lift up.

*Engaged*

It takes some maneuvering, but once she's next to me, she speaks. "Was it a tornado?"

I peek out the window and shake my head. Trees are down all around us. "I think it was a microburst. Feels like a tornado, but the wind goes in a straight line. You can tell by how the trees fall."

"We need to get out of here."

I bite my lip as I gaze at the damage. I'm not even sure the door will open. "Let me look around first." The door opens, a blessing. My eyes zero in on the ATV. The root of a hemlock rests squarely in the middle of our only motorized way out of here. I turn around and head back inside, Jenna's wide eyes focus on me.

"How bad is it out there?"

I take a deep breath. "It isn't good. A tree fell on the ATV."

Bitterness laces her words. "Oh, great. Now we have to walk home."

"Jenna, I don't think it's a good idea. Trees are down everywhere. More will fall. I think we're safer here."

She rocks back and forth as she wraps herself in the blanket. "No one knows we're here."

I want to fall on the couch and cry. If she wasn't pregnant, I'd be tempted to eat both the cookies. "We're in Speculator Falls. People will figure it out fast, it's not a big place."

"These woods are."

I don't want to debate her, and as I look around to find anything that might help, I see a two way radio. "Hey, I found something."

I dash over to the table and hold it up for her to see.

She sits up. "This is good. Ben has the other one at work. He has it in case Sara comes here. It's top of the line. I can increase wattage, so if the trees are interfering with a good signal, I think we can get a boost."

My breathing starts to even. "Great. Let's turn it on and let him know we're okay." I march to the couch and hand the device to her.

Jenna turns some buttons and knobs, then presses down on the side. "Ben? Ben? I'm at the cabin with Trish. I'm ok."

She waits and a static-filled response filters through. "Jenna? Cabin? Coming. Wayne."

We exchange looks, and Jenna pushes the button again. "What? Yes, I'm at the cabin. What about Wayne?"

His answer is faint, but we get the message. "Wayne and I are on the way to the cabin."

Engaged

# Chapter Thirty-One

Jenna opens up the baggie and hands me a cookie. "Our heroes are on the way."

My throat's dry, but I'm not rejecting the treat. "Yours is. Wayne isn't mine." Not anymore.

She brushes the crumbs off her grandmother-in-law's blanket. "Oh, stop. You two will get back together. I can feel it."

I roll my eyes. "Like you felt the storm coming?"

She tilts her head toward the window. "It's bad out there, isn't it?"

There's no way I'm pointing out that I can still hear trees falling. "It might take the guys a long time to get here. My guess is they will have to chainsaw their way."

Jenna glances at the clock on the table. "It's late afternoon. When do you think they will arrive?"

"Tonight." Maybe.

She struggles to stand and waddles over to the small kitchen area, pulling out a can of deodorizer. "This place smells terrible. If they aren't going to be meeting us right away, I guess we need to make ourselves at home."

Great.

The first thing Jenna does to waste time is take out the Bivins/Regan journal. John and Sara Bivins started the tradition when they moved in as newlyweds, writing something every day. Once it became a hunting cabin, guests wrote an entry each visit. I have several entries from high school dates with Ben.

I sit on the couch next to her. "Do you really want to read that?"

Jenna turns a yellowed page without looking at me. "Yes. This is where Ben and I had our first kiss."

I cough. "It's also where Ben and I kissed for the first time."

She scowls and tosses the book on the floor. "What do you suggest we do to pass time? It's not like we have electricity here. No television. And don't mention playing cards, because I don't want to."

I wrap my arms around my bended knees. "Let's talk about your sister and Kyle."

Jenna reaches behind her back and tosses a crocheted pillow at my face. "Not interested."

"C'mon. They really seem to like each other. I think Kyle's changing, Meg, too."

She picks at the fringe on the blanket. "He hurt Ben deeply. You know the things he's done."

A stab of regret pierces my heart. "I do. I'm among the victims, too. You sit in the same church services that preach grace and forgiveness. Can't you give him a second chance?"

"She's my only sister. This is the first person she's dating after college. I'm afraid."

Another pang. I never enjoyed being an only child. "I'm no expert given my choices and how I can't make up my mind lately, but God has Meg, and you. He knows all her days. You need to let God take care of her."

Her laugh sounds sarcastic. "That's my fear. What if His answer is Kyle stays part of her life?"

I stand and walk to the kitchen in search of some soup cans. At least with a camp stove around I can make some soup for dinner. "Pray."

Our girl talk continues through a shared can of beef vegetable, and past sunset. Jenna's eyes have dark circles around them, and mine probably do, too.

I reach for a faded yellow blanket that Ben probably used when he was in elementary school. "It looks like the guys might not get here until morning. You take the couch, and I'll go up in the loft."

Jenna sits up. "The loft is so small."

"It has a single air mattress up there, or at least it used to. I'll be fine."

She peeks at the window. "What if a tree falls?"

I shrug. "How about we pray together? I'll start, and you finish."

Her eyes close, and I fear she'll fall asleep. After a slight pause, her bold prayer wafts through the cabin. "Heavenly Father, thank You for Trish and her friendship. We give You praise for keeping us safe, and ask that You continue to. Help Ben and Wayne arrive soon, and keep them from danger. In Christ's name, Amen."

"Thank You, God, for knowing what's best for us. We trust You with our trip home. The timing, and transportation. Keep Jenna and the baby safe. Help Wayne and Ben. Give Meg and Kyle Your wisdom and understanding. May Your hand be on everyone in Speculator Falls. In the precious name of Jesus. Amen."

We open our eyes, and I notice a yellow flicker outside the window. Jenna looks to me, and I gesture for her to be still while I sneak forward. Just as I reach the door and turn the knob, I feel resistance on the other side.

I hold the knob with all my cookie infused energy. "Someone's trying to come in."

A deep voice interrupts. "Jenna, it's Ben. Let me in."

I loosen my grip and allow the men to enter. Ben looks right past me and races to the couch, where he pulls Jenna into an embrace. Wayne steps inside wearing a windbreaker and holding an industrial flashlight in hand.

Ben stands. "Thank God you two are okay."

Jenna's crying so hard she can't speak, so he sits next to her and holds her hand.

Wayne turns off the flashlight. "We had to take two of Will's ATV's because they can drive through anything. Ben was smart and packed the chainsaw. We had to cut our way here."

"Thanks for the rescue. Didn't they need you at work?"

He nods. "I'm not on the schedule, but I called and offered to look for lost hikers and campers. I didn't know you two were here until I was at the store making sure Ben and everyone inside was okay. First sign of light I'm going in the chopper to look for people."

Jenna maneuvers herself so she can stand. "Let's get going. I want civilization."

Wayne looks to Ben, who turns to his wife. "Sweetheart, we can't leave now. It's too dark."

She laughs, but it's shaky and high-pitched, her eyes wide. "Well, tell the baby."

Ben pales and I'm pretty sure if Wayne had not reached out to steady me, I'd be on the floor.

"You guys, my water just broke."

# Chapter Thirty-Two

The first thing I do is look at the floor where Jenna stands. "Okay, that's going to need a scrubbing."

She puts her hands on her hips. "Not funny."

Ben starts pacing. "Wayne, we have to get her out of here."

Wayne puts the flashlight down and saunters over. "Let's see what's going on before we panic."

I look at Wayne. "Too late."

Jenna takes a deep breath. "What do you need from me?"

His voice stays steady. "Go to the bathroom and check for more fluid. Let me know what color you see. If you have a feminine product you can use, do that, to catch any further liquids."

Jenna shuffles away, with Ben close behind. She stops and turns to him. "I can do this part alone."

He nods and re-joins Wayne and me. "Tell me they're going to be okay."

Wayne taps Ben's arm. "They will. My guess is she's one of the ten percent that has the water break, and then labor. That could start now, or in hours. She hasn't shown any signs other than the fluid. If that's the case, it's the best situation given the circumstances."

Hearing Wayne transition to work mode raises my heartbeat.

Jenna returns as if it was any other trip to the bathroom. "Clear color."

Wayne smiles. "That's what I wanted to hear. Are you feeling any contractions?"

She shakes her head. "Nothing new. I've had Braxton Hicks for a few days, but that's all they are."

Wayne glances at each of us. "Okay. The plan is stay here until daybreak. I'll radio the health center if I can reach them, and make sure once we're out of the woods that Jenna has a ride ready to transport her."

His plan sounds good to me, and Jenna nods, slipping her hand in Ben's. He stares at the floor.

"Ben, if I had any concerns, I'd tell you."

Jenna smiles. "Thanks, Wayne. I'm nervous, but not because we're stuck in a cabin. It's more of an, 'Oh my goodness, we're going to have a baby!'"

Ben looks up. "I don't think I'm going to get any sleep tonight."

Three hours later, Jenna's still traveling to the bathroom to change products, but insists she feels fine. Ben leans up against the couch, unwilling to leave her side. Wayne and I sit at the kitchen table, a flashlight our ambience.

Wayne stifles a yawn.

"Take the loft. There's a mattress there. You need the sleep. Each hour that passes means active labor is closer. We need you to be on your 'A' game."

He opens his mouth, but closes it. Then speaks. "You're handling this crisis well, Trish. You've come a long way since that race at Indian Lake."

I chuckle, trying to keep my voice low in case the parents-to-be are able to fall asleep. "That feels like years ago, not months. I confess, God's done a big change in my life lately."

Wayne rests his elbows on the wooden table. "I'd love to hear more."

His velvety voice sends shivers through me. "I finally have peace. I'm not worried about everything like I used to be. Ed Sterling was supposed to call weeks ago, and I've heard nothing. I'm okay with it, knowing it's all in God's timing."

The light hits Wayne's eyelashes just right. "That's great. I know direction for your career has been a priority for you."

I close my eyes, knowing he's right, and it played a part in our demise. "The real quest has been surrendering my dreams for God's plans. With that, I'm okay with whatever comes next. Even if I take over the department store."

Slowly, Wayne's hand inches across the table. "Can I ask a question?"

I swallow hard. "Sure."

"Do you miss us?"

He asks in such a low, romantic voice I nearly forget we're stuck in the woods with Ben and Jenna and her leaking pregnancy water. His calloused hand finds mine and I squeeze.

"I do. I'm sorry I acted so crazy and didn't listen to you."

Wayne leaves the chair and is suddenly kneeling next to me, his hand on my hair, his thumb caressing my cheek. "I apologize for not being more sensitive. I realize now how deeply hurt you were returning here, and scared for the future. I didn't make things easier."

My throat feels like I ate a package of crackers and washed it down with peanut butter. "It's okay."

Wayne leans in, his chest against mine as his lips find mine. The kiss is short, because I remember Jenna and Ben are mere feet away.

He moves back, and stands. "I think the loft is a good idea. Is that okay?"

"Yeah, probably for the best. I'll find a chair."

Wayne starts for the stairs. "Wake me if anything changes."

Sleep is non-existent as I listen to what I assume is Jenna's snoring and more trees falling around us. When the first birds start to chirp, I stretch and try to stand. Floor creaks echo throughout the downstairs from the loft.

Wayne climbs down the knotty pine steps. "Everyone okay?"

Ben stands, moving his neck back and forth, making cracking noises as he does. "I think she slept."

Jenna groans and attempts to sit up. "Can we go now?"

Wayne nods. "Yes. How are you feeling?"

Jenna places her hands on her stomach. "I didn't sleep. I was counting."

Ben furrows his brow. "What? Why were you doing that?"

She bites her lip and closes her eyes for a moment. "Counting time in-between contractions."

# Chapter Thirty-Three

Three days later, I walk into the Gloversville maternity nursing station and greet Stephanie, the nurse on duty. "Any news yet? Are we even sure there's a baby in there?"

The thirty-something woman with curly black hair laughs. "No baby yet."

Ben rounds a corner looking disheveled with a four-day beard growth and bloodshot eyes. "Trish. You've been here every day. You're a good friend."

I give him a quick hug. "After riding through the forest on those vehicles with Jenna having contractions, I feel like we're all going to be best friends."

He chuckles and runs a hand through his hair. "Good point. Doctor took her off Pitocin for good. She's still at 3cm. They're getting the surgery team ready for a C-section."

"Wow. How's Jenna?"

"Tired. Ready to meet our baby. I want a quick cup of coffee before they take her. Are you staying?"

Wayne's on duty, so I don't have anything going on. The college girls have the store open. Mom and Dad are back at the office. "Sure. Want anything?"

He nods. "Could you call Pastor and Brooke? They visited yesterday and I promised to call with any updates."

"Absolutely. I'll be praying."

Ben flashes a grin. "Thanks, Trish."

I take a seat in the waiting room and sign-in with the hospital WI-FI. The microburst is the lead story in all news outlets based in the Adirondacks. The event so rare in the season and path, yet no fatalities. Sara let the Speculator Falls residents know that most of the tree damage was confined to the forest. I haven't stopped counting my blessings since we left the woods.

Wayne's woodsy cologne enters the waiting room before he does. He wastes no time walking over and giving me a quick kiss on the mouth. "I thought I'd find you here. I just finished a transport, and need to drive back. I do have news."

I put my phone on the end table. "About Jenna?"

He shakes his head. "I wish. Work."

Curiosity spikes. "What's going on?"

"Brad and Jill were fired. Turns out Jill was my partner because she and Brad were both found negligent of duty. They were sneaking off instead of working. They were written up but given another chance. When the storm hit, Brad was on duty and they called Jill in when I let them know I was stuck in the forest. They were found on a road with tree damage. Instead of calling it in for the road crew or trying to chainsaw through, they used it as a private place to drink and be 'chummy.'"

Color me sad. Not. "Wow. That's pretty selfish. That means more work for you, right?" I reach for his hand.

Wayne nods. "Don't worry, I'll make sure we have plenty of time together. You won't even have to faint." He kisses my hand and stands. "I hate to say it, but I have to go back. I'll pray for Jenna as I drive. She's a strong one, that's for sure."

I rise and kiss his cheek, but he turns so that our lips touch. "I wish you didn't have to go."

"Me too. The good news is neither of us are going anywhere. I should be off Sunday. Noah wants to grill and have you over."

It's a beautiful image. Wayne, Noah, and me. "It's a date."

He leaves one quick peck on the cheek and walks to the door before turning to me. "Trish, I love you."

My heart receives his declaration as I choke up. "I love you, too."

⧗⧗⧗

An hour later, Sara, Meg, Kyle, Pastor Reynolds and Brooke join me in the waiting room. Sara lifts her knitting needles out of her bag and goes to work while Meg wears out the carpet with her pacing.

Kyle reaches for a magazine at the end table close to me. "I heard you were caught up in the microburst."

I search his eyes for any hint of mockery or manipulation. "We were, but thankfully, the only damage was to an ATV. Any worry we had about Jenna having the baby at the cabin is a joke now."

His laugh is soft. "I guess. She could be in the Guinness Book of Records."

Before I can respond, Ben rushes in, panting. "Boy! It's a boy!"

Meg squeals and runs to Kyle, who opens his arms for a warm hug.

Pastor Reynolds raises his hands in a praise gesture. "Wonderful news. Congratulations."

Brooke stands. "What's his name? Is Jenna okay?"

Ben nods, takes a tissue from the coffee table and dabs his eyes. "They're both perfect. I'm a dad. I can't believe it."

I put my hands on my hips. "So, what's his name?"

He laughs. "Sorry, I'm a mess. His name is John Bivins Regan."

Sara puts her hands to her mouth for a moment. "Ben, what a way to honor your grandfather."

He walks over to her. "We didn't even have to think about what to name a son. I hope we raise John as well as my parents, as you and Grandpa raised me."

She pats his shoulder. "You will."

Ben jogs to the door. "The doctor said she can have two visitors. Grandma? Meg?"

Sara smiles. "Oh, dear, you and Meg can go in. I'm here all day. I can go whenever."

He looks to his sister-in-law. "Meg, Kyle? Would you like to see John?"

Meg's eyes brighten as she holds Kyle's arm. "We'd love to."

⌛⌛⌛

While the Regan family recovers and gets to know each other, everyone at church talks about Jenna and the baby before service.

Shirley acts as Jenna's publicist and shares with Mabel John's weight, length, and how his first bath went.

Wayne elbows my side. "You'd think she's the grandmother."

"In a way, she kind of is. I never took advantage of the perks of the senior center job. Jenna's able to have grandparents galore there. With the baby, she's never going to have a second to herself."

After worship and announcements, Pastor Reynolds places his Bible on the pulpit. "I promise, I wrote this message before Jenna went into labor. It's about finishing strong."

Everyone giggles. Wayne opens up his Bible and gets out a pencil, scribbling on the note section of his bulletin. He nudges me, and I glance at the paper.

*We're going to finish strong. I love you.*

Be still my heart.

Later that afternoon, Wayne's grilling steaks for us. Noah's girlfriend, Olivia, wearing her charm bracelet, joins us. As we gather around the picnic table with corn on the cob, tossed salad, and baked potatoes, my phone rings.

I stare at the screen, not answering.

Wayne looks over from the grill. "Who is it?"

"Ed Sterling."

Noah listens to another ring before he swings his arms. "Answer it, Trish! You've been waiting for that guy to call for like, ever."

Right. I need to actually swipe to answer, not just stare. "Hello, Mr. Sterling?"

His tenor voice comes through clearly. "Miss Maxwell, I owe you an apology."

"You do?"

He clears his throat. "Yes. First, for calling on a Sunday. I never received your phone message from a month ago. I don't know what happened, but when my secretary heard me mention your name, she asked if I called you back. I had no idea. I wanted to call Monday, but with the latest news, I thought I'd call sooner."

I look at Wayne and shrug. "It's okay. I assumed you weren't interested in my work."

"Quite the contrary. I have a business acquaintance that you know, Kyle Swarthmore, and he was raving about you during a meeting. He told me you were even setting up store front displays in Lake Schroon. Lake Placid. Saranac Lake. That's impressive."

I cough as soon as I hear Kyle's kind gesture, but recover. Miracles never cease. "Thank you, sir."

"It sounds like you have a lot more experience, and that was a concern before. We also received news today regarding funds."

My hands are so wet I almost drop my cell. "Really?"

"We received a grant notice, and it's one we hoped would come through so we could partner with you. We're also writing one now for emergency storm relief. Although your area in Speculator Falls wasn't hard hit in business areas, not everywhere in the Adirondacks can say the same. We hope additional funds can be used to beautify the business districts affected by the storms."

I turn away from Noah because he's making dramatic gestures with his arms and face trying to get me to laugh. That kid.

"That's great, Mr. Sterling. May I ask what this has to do with me?"

"I can't promise beyond a year, but we have the money in place to give you a small salary and monies for supplies if you're interested in working through the Greater Adirondack Chamber."

It takes everything not to jump up and down and scream. "That's wonderful! I would love it."

"Excellent. I won't tie up anymore of your Sunday, but call me tomorrow morning at the office. Let's get moving right away."

Engaged

# Chapter Thirty-Four

The church gym air conditioning doesn't help much as Wayne and I get our activity tracker steps in while decorating for Dad's retirement party. The red, white, and blue balloon arch gives a patriotic flair even though it's July 5th.

Wayne balances his side of the arch. "How many people are coming?"

I wipe my brow with my arm. "I have 122 RSVP's."

He pauses. "Wow. I hope Wendy made enough potato salad."

"That's the least of my worries. I rented extra chairs and they aren't here yet. Sara's baking the cake but it's so humid, I wonder if the icing will melt."

Wayne steps back and strides over to me. He holds out a hand and lifts me up and into his embrace. "Trish, it's going to be an amazing day. Your parents are healthy and now have time to travel, volunteer, do whatever they want. They aren't going to focus on party basics." He kisses me several times before we indulge in one longer kiss.

Will opens the doors. "Chairs are here."

I break off the kiss, but give my man a wink. "Thanks, Will. We'll be right there to unload."

After we arrange the chairs, Sara arrives with the cake. Wendy and her sons bring in the catered food. Preparations go so fast I don't have time to change before guests start to arrive.

Shirley's the first, and she brings a gift bag. "Trish, you look like Cinderella before Prince Charming."

I bite my lip. My senior friend will never be at a loss for words.

Wayne glances at the clock. "Go in the ladies room and change. Your parents aren't here yet. Noah and I can handle greetings."

I pause, but Shirley tilts her head in the direction of the bathroom. "Okay. Knock on the door if any of the village board members arrive. I have special seating for them."

# Engaged

Ten minutes later, I walk out with a dusty rose sundress on and my hair fresh with beachy curl spray. I balance my trek in high heels across the gym floor as honeysuckle perfume surrounds me. Just as I find Wayne, Noah cups his hands together.

"Trish, your parents are here!"

I take a deep breath and look around. The decorations transform the gym into a fun party atmosphere. Dad's law colleagues and clients are here. His fellow board members. My uncle from Vermont. Church friends. Even his friends from college made the trip.

Wayne squeezes my shoulders, and I realize how wound tight I am with his touch. "This is amazing. You did a great job. Go introduce your parents."

I nod and move to the arch. Pastor Reynolds hands me a microphone.

Dad and Mom are holding hands, dad in a tuxedo, and mom in a red sleeveless dress. When our eyes meet, they stroll over and wrap me in a hug.

I whisper so the microphone can't pick up my voice. "Congratulations. I'm so happy for you both."

Mom's eye makeup starts to smear as tears fall. "We owe it to you."

I lift the microphone to my mouth. "Ladies and gentlemen…" There's no amplification, so I turn it upside down and click the button. "Ladies and…" Still no power.

Wayne saunters over. "Can I help?"

I pass the microphone over to him. "Yes, it isn't working."

He holds it for a second before he hands it over to my dad.

I look at him like he has two heads. "Wayne, it isn't working. I need to introduce them."

Wayne doesn't answer. He gets on one knee, and Noah joins him, doing the same.

A crowd gathers around us as I freeze. My mouth refuses to move. My feet follow suit.

Wayne opens a black velvet box. "Trish Maxwell, when you came to town, it wasn't where you wanted to be. But it was where God wanted you, and we're so glad. I love you. I love how you tried to run a race even though you aren't a runner. That you're passionate about your talent. You're a great friend, and now, a wonderful babysitter." He glances at Ben, Jenna, and Baby John, before returning his gaze on me. "I believe you'll be an amazing wife."

Noah's words tumble like a toddler in gym class. "Will you marry us?

The applause is so loud it mimics the microburst, but I'm not scared.

Although my feet feel like they have cement blocks attached out of pure shock, I step toward them. "You guys. How did you pull this off?

Mom waves. "What better way to pull off a proposal than distract you with a retirement party?"

That's for sure.

Noah looks at the box. "Well? Are you in, or out?"

I stand in front of them, nodding. "I'm so in."

Through more hand-clapping Wayne slips the ring on my finger and we kiss. I reach for Noah and give him a hug. "I love you two so much."

Wayne kisses me again. "I love you. And we need to marry, soon." He winks.

Noah asks for the microphone and whatever Pastor Reynolds did to make it not work for me, suddenly works as the teen speaks. "Hey everybody, we're engaged!"

# Engaged

# If you loved Engaged...

**It would mean a lot if you would leave a review on Amazon and Goodreads.** It takes a couple minutes of your time and makes a world of difference. *The more reviews that are on Amazon, the more exposure a book receives.*

If you aren't sure what to write when leaving a review, include a couple standout moments you enjoyed without giving the plot away, and don't mention knowing the author if you do. If a reader sees that a reviewer wrote that the author is a friend or something similar, the reader thinks the review isn't accurate.

# Thank you!

I appreciate you reading ENGAGED. If you're struggling because your dreams aren't matching up with God's plans, be encouraged. He is a good Heavenly Father who wants the very best for you. I have learned more than once when something I wanted didn't work out, it was because God had something so much better in store. As scary as it is, you will find freedom through surrender. Trust Him today!

Engaged

# COMING 2018:

## *Surrendering Opinions Series*

Six siblings are thrust in the national spotlight at birth and kept there by tragic circumstances. They grow up with a lot of help around them. As young adults, they each try to discover their identities and find a romance as strong as what their parents had.

A six book series about surrendering what others think.

Enjoy a sneak peek from Book 1, tentatively titled ANCHORED.

Anchored

# Anchored
## Prologue

### 1992

Julia Turmeric stared at the cordless phone in her hand. The buzz of the newsroom swarmed around her, but her focus remained on the disconnected call.

A set of finger snaps brought her back to reality. "Jules! What's going on? I've been talking to you about Hussein's latest statement and I didn't even get an eye roll."

She turned her head to Walt Crawford, her favorite cameraman, and held up the phone. "It's my best friend from back home, Lisa Collins."

Her colleague nodded. "Oh, right. The morning anchor at that little station Upstate, right?"

Julia bit her lip as she replaced the phone to the base. "Yeah. She's pregnant."

"I remember you saying something about it, that she and the husband had been trying for a while. She okay?"

Her expression still vacant, she sighed. "They just learned they are carrying sextuplets. I knew they were doing infertility treatments and there was a chance of multiples, but this?" She ran a finger through her long, ebony, straight hair. "The doctors asked them to reduce, she had some term for it, but she's real serious about her faith. Very pro-life."

He picked up a tripod. "She's keeping all of them?"

She tapped the camera. "And Lisa wants us to document their story."

### December, 1992

Julia unbuckled the seatbelt and stared at the ranch-style home in front of her. "How are Lisa and Paul taking care of six babies in this little house?"

Walt took the keys out of the ignition and shrugged. "This is your old Big Flats neighborhood, right? You grew up in a house like this with brothers and sisters."

She pulled down the visor mirror and applied fresh lipstick. "Not six born at once." She snapped the visor back in place and blotted her mouth with a tissue. "If anyone can do this, it's Lisa. That girl could make the hardest person smile and tell their story to her for the camera. I still don't understand how she didn't keep our pact. In college we said we'd go national together."

"Love will do it all the time." He chuckled. "Ask my ex-wives."

Julia rolled her eyes and gestured toward the house. "Can you get some exterior shots? I'm going in."

She closed her eyes for a moment and took a deep breath before ringing the doorbell. Julia recognized Lisa's mom, Gail, when she opened the door, cradling a baby.

Gail's smile was wide. "If it isn't little JT from down the street. Come in."

Julia remembered the childhood name for Lisa's mom. "Hi, Mama G. Who do you have here?"

Gail's shaky laugh echoed in the entry. "If he didn't have a tag, I wouldn't know. This is James Matthew Collins, number four out of six."

Six babies still seemed so surreal. Julia looked down the hall and could see a swing in motion.

"My cameraman will be inside soon. We have a lot to do. Can I see Paul and Lisa?"

Mama G. nodded and strolled down the hall to what Julia guessed was a living room. The couch and TV were there, but everything else was baby related. Swings. Baby chairs. Cradles.

Julia could barely take it all in. Two people were in front of her on the couch, each holding a baby. On the floor a woman sat near the swings, watching the remaining three fight sleep as they rocked back and forth.

Gail lowered her voice. "Lisa, Paul, Julia's here."

The two rose from the couch and faced Julia. Lisa navigated through the maze of equipment to reach her friend. "Julia! Thank you so much for doing this. It means everything to Paul and me that you're the one covering our journey."

Julia leaned in for a quick hug. "Are you kidding? Do you know how many stations around the world want to interview the parents of the multiples who not only refused selective reduction but also had them stay the longest in the womb? You are all medical miracles."

Lisa glanced at Paul, who was at her side. "It's all God. He blessed and took care of us."

Paul chuckled. "And we pray He keeps providing. We need all the help we can get."

### July 1995

Julia touched the ends of her newly-cut hair. The humidity in New York City seemed extra miserable, but the five hour trek to Corning didn't seem to provide any relief. The short hair took getting used to, but she was glad she did it.

Walt shook his head as the Collins home came into view. "Look at all the tricycles."

"It's crazy. At least that means the kids are more mobile than the first time we met them. I can't believe the community pitched in and had this home built for them."

He nodded and pulled into the long, blacktop driveway. Three of the kids were in the yard blowing bubbles. "Viewers eat this up. They love this family. Lisa was smart to lock you in as lifetime interviewer no matter what job you have, or what station."

Julia smiled. Lisa may have left the news business for home life with the kids, but she was savvy. Every year the media sent Paul and Lisa publicity requests to see the kids and interview them. Lisa found a lawyer willing to draft an exclusive agreement that gave Julia the only access to what reporters called the kids, 'The Collins Six.'

"And now that I'm co-anchor of *Rise and Shine*, I think ratings will skyrocket. Moms watch the show, and they adore Lisa." Julia reached for her briefcase and looked out the window. "Speaking of, here she is."

Lisa sauntered over to the news van, her long hair piled on top of her head. "Julia. Walt. It can't be another year already."

The two exited the vehicle and greeted *Faces and Places* magazine's Mom of the Year with a hug. "What's three years old like? Does it get worse than terrible two?" Walt opened the back of the van.

Lisa shook her head. "All I can say is if your producer wants a transparent look at 'The Collins Six,' you're going to have plenty of footage."

Julia heard a screech, followed by a cry. One of the boys held an empty bubble bottle while one of the girls had wet, soapy hair. Julia tapped her favorite cameraman. "You can start by taping that."

**September 1997**

Julia tripped over a backpack on her way to the spacious Collins kitchen. Jimmy and Jill, babies four and five, were eating at the kitchen table. "Hey, guys. Can I ask you a couple questions?"

Jimmy looked to his sister, then to Julia. "Is it for TV?"

She nodded.

He narrowed his eyes and took another bite. "Are you gonna ask about school?"

Julia smiled. "Yes, that's what everyone wants to know about."

He put the bread on a plate. "I can make it easy. We all hate it."

Julia bit her lip to kill the temptation to laugh. She glanced at Jill, who nodded. "Hate it."

**January 2001**

Julia placed a piece of hair behind her ear as she looked at notes for her upcoming interview with the latest A-lister actress. The morning show and evening magazine duties gave her a lot of assignments with Hollywood's elite, but few gave Julia joy in prepping for the meeting.

She took a sip of her coffee and heard a knock on the door. Glancing at her office clock, it was late in the evening for visitors. "Who is it?"

His voice cracked. "Walt."

Julia stood and jogged to the door. He was always home and with his family once his assignments were done. She opened it, ready to invite him in, when she saw his hands shake and his eyes full of tears. "What's wrong?"

"I told the brass I would be the one to tell you."

Her eyebrows furrowed as she tried to discern what he was saying.

"Julia, there's been a terrible accident back in your hometown."

She felt the pit form and enlarge as she instantly thought of her parents and siblings. "Dad? Mom?"

Walt shook his head. "Lisa and a couple of the kids."

Julia felt her knees sliding beneath her. "Tell me they are okay."

She never, in all her years choosing Walt as her cameraman, saw him cry.

"Lisa's gone."

# Anchored

# Acknowledgements

I learned with this series that with each book theme, it will be tested through the author. This time around I found myself battling anxiety as I feared for the future. There were two deaths that shocked me to the core. There were changes in and around our children that made me want to figure their futures out. This book was borne out of sweat, tears, coffee smoothies, and prayer.

My Prayer Covering team, you know who you are, your prayers rescued me from delay, discouragement, and detours. This year marked ten years a group of women have been praying for me, and some of you have been praying all ten years. My thanks to Brenda and Shirley for reaching that milestone with me. Jennifer, like Christ, you made praying for this ministry look like it was the only thing you served in. I knew it wasn't, but well done, faithful servant, well done. You are so missed. Until we meet again.

My thanks to Scribes 202 and Scribes 210 for their critiques. You make writing look easy. Members changed throughout the series, but every single author helped make the series readable.

Kim Bilas, you were an answer to prayer with your editing. Julie Brown and Holly Hrywnak, thank you for being such faithful BETA readers throughout the series.

Pastor Gary Gray, thank you for permission to use notes from your sermons in my work.

Holly, Aiden, and Maddy, thank you for the input and encouragement. Thanks Aiden, for letting me borrow most of your name for a character.

The CIA (Christian Indie Author) Facebook group, thank you for the treasure trove of information. Elizabeth Maddrey for formatting help

Hannah Arduini, Tom Nuttall and the Entangled book club ladies, thank you for the accountability. Summer, Linda, Rhonda, and Deb, thank you for sharing any book news I had.

Mom, for supporting me in every possible way.

Crista, Landon, Mandy, Randy, Matt, and Stephanie, for being great cheerleaders. Oliver and James, for being the best grandsons we could pray for.

Tom, Brian, and Hannah, for believing in the call on my life and encouraging me when I was tired and depressed.

To the One I trust with all my heart who helps me lean not on my own understanding, thank You for making my path straight.

# The Surrendering Time Series

**Entrusted:** Surrendering the Present is a **FREE eRead** at http://juliearduini.com or purchase on Amazon.

**Entangled:** Surrendering the Past is available for purchase on Amazon.

**Engaged:** Surrendering the Future is what you're reading now!

**Finding Freedom Through Surrender**---A 30 Day Devotional takes the themes and characters from the series to encourage your surrender journey. Available for purchase on Amazon.

**Stay in touch** with me through http://juliearduini.com, follow me on Amazon and Goodreads to learn about free book opportunities and giveaways. I also love to connect through social media. Find me and say hi @JulieArduini!

Julie Arduini, Heidi Glick, Elizabeth Maddrey, Kym McNabney, Paula Mowery, Donna Winters

A *Walk* in the *Valley*

Christian encouragement for your journey through *Infertility*

edited by Lynellen D.S. Perry, PhD

"This is the book I wish I had when I was going through the heartbreak and bitterness that was my infertility. It was an honor to share my story with these other authors, who express their experiences with transparency and hope." ---Julie Arduini

With questions designed to journal your own journey, A WALK IN A VALLEY is for anyone going through infertility, including loved ones wondering how they can help.

**Available on Amazon in Print and Kindle Editions.**
Don't have a Kindle? Download the FREE Amazon app and start reading on your electronic device.

# Stay Encouraged and Informed with

## Surrendered Scribe Media/

## Julie Arduini

- FREE e-Read of ENTRUSTED, Book 1 in Surrendering Time Series.
- Exclusive news, encouragement, giveaways, freebies.
- No crowding your inbox. Monthly updates with encouragement just for you!

## To receive your free e-Copy of Entrusted subscribe:

http://eepurl.com/dCFG or at juliearduini.com.

## Follow Inspy Romance:

Blog:

http://inspyromance.com

Twitter:

https://twitter.com/inspyromance

Facebook:

https://facebook.com/inspyromance

Pinterest:

https://pinterest.com/inspyromance

# Regan's Acts of Kindness

Although I never met Regan, her parents spent a lot of time with us when we lived in Upstate NY. Regan was taken from them in January 2017. She would have turned four in March.

Everyone who loves Regan wants her to be remembered. Regan's Acts of Kindness is one way to accomplish this.

**Please like Regan's Acts of Kindness on Facebook,** http://facebook.com/RegansActsOfKindness, print out the flyer, and do kind things.

**Donations can be made to Regan's Memorial Fund:**

http://youcaring.com/reganshetsky

Thank you!

# About the Author

Julie Arduini loves to encourage readers to surrender the good, the bad, and ---maybe one day---the chocolate. She's the author of the Surrendering Time series (*Entrusted*, *Entangled*, and *Engaged*.) She also shared her story in the infertility devotional workbook/journal, *A Walk in the Valley*. She blogs every other Wednesday for Christians Read and monthly for Inspy Romance. Originally from Upstate New York, she resides in Ohio with her husband and two children. Learn more by visiting her at http://juliearduini.com and connecting with her @JulieArduini throughout social media, including Amazon and Goodreads.

www.ingramcontent.com/pod-product-compliance
Lightning Source LLC
Chambersburg PA
CBHW061145170626
46809CB00003B/990